AnneMa

CW00395059

First Publication: Septemb
under the author name Anne Whitfield.
Cover design by Image: AnneMarie Brear

1

Broken Hero

Historical

Kitty McKenzie
Kitty McKenzie's Land
Southern Sons
To Gain What's Lost
Isabelle's Choice
Nicola's Virtue
Aurora's Pride
Grace's Courage
Eden's Conflict
Catrina's Return
Where Rainbow's End
Broken Hero
The Promise of Tomorrow
The Slum Angel

Marsh Saga Series

Millie
Christmas at the Chateau
Prue
Cece

Contemporary

Long Distance Love
Hooked on You
Where Dragonflies Hover (Dual Timeline)

Short Stories

A New Dawn
Art of Desire
What He Taught Her

AnneMarie Brear

Broken Hero

Chapter One

East Yorkshire, England
Spring, 1944

Audrey wiped the sweat from her brow and arched her back to stretch the cramping muscles. The cold wind coming from the ocean blew her hair into her eyes, making her shiver as the beaded sweat dried cool on her skin.

She glared at the conked-out old tractor. A small sprout of steam erupted from its engine's pipes and hissed before it lay quiet.

'Damn! Blast!' Audrey slapped the top of the tractor and glanced to the uneven ploughed field sloping away down the hill. Potatoes. An acre of potatoes she had to plant and in the next field would be turnips. Same as last year. Same hard work, same relentless monotony. But soon it would be summer and if she had to work hard, she'd rather do it with the sun on her back than the artic winds of winter.

'You all right then, luv?' A young man wearing brown corduroy civilian clothes, with a bag slung over his shoulder, cycled to a stop and hopped off his bicycle. 'What's the problem?' He peered over the dry-stone wall at her, a cheeky grin flashed.

Pulling her coat tightly around her, Audrey looked at him with a wry lift of her eyebrow. He wasn't a soldier or looked like a simple postman. 'As you can see,' she hooked a thumb at the hissing tractor, 'I can't get the thing going again.'

'Aye, right.' He nodded and studied the old machine with interest.

'Do you know anything about fixing them?' She asked hopefully, looking up at the low grey sky, and praying it wouldn't rain again.

'Well, not tractors exactly. I'm more of a motor-bike man.' He grinned again, showing his white teeth. 'There's no call for those machines in the streets of my old hometown of Newcastle, I'm afraid. I'm not used to country things.'

Audrey sighed. Typical. He was the first able-bodied man under eighty she'd seen for months, and he wouldn't know a tractor from a cow. She glanced at the temperamental machine, not liking it that much. She now understood why Owen preferred the horse and plough. 'Oh. Well then, I'd best get on.'

'But I believe an engine is an engine.' He winked. 'Let me have a look at it.'

'Really? I do appreciate it.'

'Sure.' He rested the bicycle against the wall and climbed over to join her.

'Thank you. I do hate taking up your time.'

'I'm in no hurry.' The fellow grinned and walked with a slight limp towards the tractor.

Audrey peered at the engine and pointed to where the steam had hissed out. 'I think the steam came from somewhere here.'

After a few minutes of frowning, touching a few things and generally looking puzzled, the young man straightened and nodded. 'There's your problem. A blown hose.' He bent and pointed at the top of the engine. 'See here? That split is the cause. It'll need replacing.'

'Blast.'

He dusted his hands together. 'I work part time at Potter's garage in Bridlington. I'll call in on the way back and see if we have a hose there that'll fit.'

Audrey walked back to the wall with him. 'Thank you. I can send one of the men in to get it.'

'If they can't manage to come in, I'll bring it out to you in a few days.' He clambered over the stones and collected his bicycle. 'You wouldn't know where Pearson's Lane is, would you?'

'You're on it.'

A look of amazement crossed his features. 'Am I? Good lord. I've been pedalling for miles wondering if I was going the right way.'

'Where are you headed?'

'Twelve Pines. You know it?'

She nodded and smiled. 'It's another mile down that way.' She gestured towards an ancient oak woodland. 'You can see the house chimneys through the trees as you go over that last bit of a rise.'

'Splendid.' He adjusted his bag and swung a leg across the bicycle.

'Why aren't you serving?' She couldn't help but ask. Seeing a young man in civilian clothes was unusual now, after four years of war. 'You're not in uniform.'

6

For a moment, his expression tightened before his grin returned. 'I'm not enlisted for active duty anymore.' He tapped his leg. 'Wounded in '40. I left half my foot on some French field.' He shrugged.

She wanted to say something soothing, like she did when she sat with the patients in the evenings, but instinct told her this man was beyond the need of smooth words and had picked himself back up and got on with living.

'Why didn't you go home to Newcastle?'

'You ask a lot of questions.'

She blushed. 'Sorry. It's a habit.'

'Nay, don't be. There's nothing for me at home. My parents died while I was in France. We used to come to Bridlington when I was a lad. So, I thought this would be a good a place as any to live for a while. When I'm not working at the garage, I'm helping the Home Guard and run errands for the army staff sometimes, when they're short of manpower.' He lifted the bag. 'Letters. This was passed to me by some army officer whose car had broken down. He paid me a shilling to deliver them. I was going to offer to look at his engine, but I doubt he'd pay me a shilling to do that, so I took the delivery job instead.'

Audrey chuckled. 'In the end you looked at *my* engine.'

He laughed. 'You're better looking than the officer.'

She couldn't help but smile at his flattery and good humour. 'When you get to Twelve Pines, go through the front door. The office is on the left. Ask for Sister Lewis, she'll help you.'

'Rightio.'

'Will you deliver more messages?'

'Depends on what staff are available. We got a hell of a raid last night. Headquarters in Brid are run ragged today.'

She'd heard the siren last night and they'd spent four hours in the cellar until the 'all clear' sounded. 'Was it bad?'

'Bad enough. Anyway, I should go. Thanks!' He pushed off, his steering a little wobbly, and waved.

Audrey watched him ride around the bend until he was lost from sight by the trees lining the road.

'Audrey!'

She turned and walked around the side of the tractor. Lucy was walking up the field, waving, and knowing she could do no more for today, Audrey gave the tractor a loathing glare and went down to meet her sister. 'Have you come to help me?'

Puffing, Lucy brushed her black curls away from her face. 'Not likely. You may enjoy getting your hands dirty, but I do not.'

'You just missed a young man on a bicycle,' she teased.

Lucy's blue eyes widened, her mouth pouting. 'Young?'

'Very eligible, I'm sure.' She nudged her with her elbow.

'Darn.' Lucy thumped her worn tweed skirt. 'I've missed another chance. What did he want?'

'Delivering a message from the army.'

'He'd not have noticed you, especially wearing that hideous brown overall you live in.'

Audrey looked down at the stained, baggy overall. It was hideous but served a purpose like most things had to do nowadays. 'It saves my clothes.'

'It makes you look odd.' Lucy sniffed.

They linked arms and headed back down the hill. Audrey eyed her younger sibling, who felt, at eighteen, her life was over because the war had taken all the good young men and either killed them or maimed them so far. 'So why have you left the house and come all this way? You hate walking anywhere.'

'Valerie wanted you home and I volunteered to come find you because I had nothing else to do. She received a letter mentioning the possibility of some new arrivals. I think she's worried we'll not fit them all in, which we won't. Father should complain.'

Audrey frowned. 'More? Why are they sending us more? We're bursting at the seams now. I don't understand why my letters are being ignored by the Army.'

'The army does as it likes, you should know that by now. They won't listen to you. They wouldn't listen to Father either.' Lucy's eyes narrowed. 'I told you we should have closed the house and gone to Canada with Aunt Flo.'

'And I told you, the army would have taken the house anyway, especially if it's empty. No, staying was all we could do, plus Father wanted it.' They reached the small coppice edging the formal gardens that no longer displayed beautiful blooms, but now were rows of vegetables.

Following the service drive, they went around the back of the house and into the large cloakroom. Max, their father's old arthritic black Labrador, wagged his tail from his basket in the corner. Audrey gave him a quick pat before changing her boots for shoes and taking her coat off. 'Do I look tidy?'

Lucy screwed up her face. 'Overalls, with no make-up and that hair, I suppose it's the best you can do.'

9

'You are so *charming*.' Audrey touched her wildly curling hair, cut short for the ease of working the numerous chores that were now hers alone.

'I'm off to find Father. His cough isn't too good today. I worry.' Lucy hung up her coat and shook out her long black curls and then efficiently tied them up again with a red ribbon. 'Call me if you need me, which you won't, as you and *Sister Lewis* are like generals when new arrivals come; all orders and frowns.'

'Ha ha.' Audrey poked her tongue out. As they parted in the hall, Audrey made for the front of the house and the little office, which had once been a small parlour. The wide entrance hall was quiet today. The patients, those who could get out of bed, stayed close by the fires in their rooms or lingered in the conservatory, which trapped any warmth the day might give.

Audrey walked in and smiled at the surprised face of the bicycle man with the toothy smile. 'You found us then?'

'Yes.' He blinked and flashed his grin. 'It's grand it was you I saw and not someone else.'

'No, you'd have been fine, as everyone knows Twelve Pines.'

'You were cheeky not to let on you worked here.'

'Yes, I know, very naughty of me. Sorry about that.' She held out her hand and shook his. 'Audrey Pearson. This is my family's home.'

He whistled low and then grinned. 'Nice to meet you. I thought you were just a land army girl. I'm—'

'Oh my.' Valerie's groan cut through the introductions.

'What?' Audrey walked behind the desk, patting Sister Valerie Lewis's shoulder as she did so. 'Is it something awful?'

'Well, this young man…Robert…has brought us official papers, confirming the letter I received this morning. We're getting new arrivals.'

Audrey glanced away from the messenger, who held the same name as her brother, a brother lost to her like so many brothers were lost across the country.

Valerie heaved a deep sigh. 'We have been assigned a new doctor, at last. Poor Doctor Penshaw will be glad of the help. He's getting too old…'

Tired, and a little weary of upheaval, Audrey sat on the edge of the desk. 'When are we to expect them?'

'Today, I believe. A doctor, patients and *two* nurses, or so this informs me. No warning, so we could prepare, of course. Obviously can't break the habit of the last year. When does the Army ever consider the rest of us?' Valerie glanced up from studying the papers. 'We're getting ten more, Audrey, *ten*. And these poor fellows are worse than we've ever had.' She shook the papers. 'We're a convalescence home, not a hospital, but they seem to have forgotten that. How will we cope?'

Audrey stared at her friend, seeing for the first time a sign of her fears at not managing a task given to her. Valerie Lewis had come to Twelve Pines with the first five men that came here to recover from their injuries, physical and mental, gained from the front-line battles. She and Audrey had become firm friends immediately. Never in the two years she'd been at the house had Valerie weakened, and for that alone Audrey would have been proud of her, but now, seeing her fragility for the first time, Audrey felt even more compassion for the wonderful young woman, who at twenty-six, was only a year older than herself.

'We will manage, Val. Of course, we will. We have no alternative.' She squeezed her shoulder. Then, aware they had an audience, she straightened and smiled at the message bearer. 'Please go to the kitchens, R-Robert, and have something to eat. Mrs Graham will fill you up.' She forced herself to smile and ignore the stammer over her brother's name.

He nodded. 'Perhaps I'll have a cup of tea before I start my ride back. Thank you kindly. And don't forget about the engine hose. Come to the garage.'

'I won't forget.'

At the door, he paused and glanced over his shoulder. 'You're both brave lasses and let no one ever tell you any different. This country wouldn't have survived like it has without our women. I know that, even if most other men will never acknowledge it.'

'Thank you.' Audrey watched the doorway long after he'd gone. He was right. Without the women working the men's jobs while they were away, the country would have suffered, but what about when the men come home again? At this thought, she forced herself to ignore her own questions. For torturing herself on what might be wouldn't help her.

'I wouldn't mind a cup of tea myself,' Valerie mumbled. 'I think we'll have a rough night of it, settling everyone in.'

Scratching her head, Audrey thought of the rooms left available to them to convert. Upstairs was full of beds, even she and Lucy shared one room now. Her father still had his room, but the few servants and nurses were in the attics, while Valerie slept on a cot bed in the linen room on the landing. An option

Audrey hated her enduring, but one that Valerie said she preferred so she could be nearer the men should they need her.

Valerie stood and went to file the papers in the cabinet by the window. 'We have the drawing room, rear parlour and the morning room. The dining room will have to remain as such, I really don't want the men who can walk to have to eat in bed. While ever we can give them some sense of normality, I'd rather continue it, and eating in a dining room gives them that.'

'I agree.' Audrey stepped towards the door. Opposite, a convalescing officer strolled into the drawing room with a newspaper under his arm. 'Come let us inspect the morning room.' She indicated to the officer. 'The men like the drawing room and they need somewhere to read and smoke in.'

Together they walked down the hall and turned left into the light sunny morning room, a room Audrey's late mother, Joanna, had liked to sit in and write her correspondence. Audrey always smiled in here, for her mother's presence was closer here than anywhere else.

Her attention was caught by a lady's magazine on the chair by the window. Lucy now used this room for her private time and would huff about another family room being taken over.

Valerie paced out the floor. 'The rug will have to go. If we move out all the furniture…We could get five beds in here at a pinch.'

Audrey ran her fingertips across her mother's elegant desk. Like most of the family's furniture and belongings, it too would be stored in the barns and outbuildings. It seemed that since the war started, all traces of her life were being eroded away. The house no longer rang of laughter and friends staying to party the weekends away. Instead, whispers seemed to linger in corners, the smell of disinfectant coated every surface and strangers walked the halls.

'Perhaps we can put another bed in with Major Johnson and Captain Watts,' Valerie said, striding to the window and inspecting the lace curtains and the horrid blackout drapes. 'These will have to be washed and the floor scrubbed.'

'Why didn't they give us more notice?' Audrey rubbed her forehead, sighing at the amount of work to be done. She'd been up since dawn and hadn't stopped all day. 'I'll get Alf and Owen to come in and take all this out into storage, then we can wash the floor.'

'There are cots in the barn. They'll have to be disinfected and perhaps we can find an old table or something to put the medical supplies on.'

'I don't think we have any more.' She chewed a fingernail. 'All the old nursery room furniture is being used.'

'Perhaps we can get some tables in Bridlington?'

Audrey nodded. 'I'll ask around when I next go into town.'

'What's that noise?' Valerie paused; her head cocked to one side. 'A car? I do hope it's our supplies. We're low on so many things.'

The loud rumble of the engines and the crunching of the wheels on the gravel drive were too much to be a single car.

'Sounds like a truck.'

'More than one.' Valerie closed her eyes. 'They're here and we're not ready.'

They left the room and hurried up the hallway to the front door. Dragging it open, Audrey groaned as they stared at the three large army ambulance trucks in the drive. The first driver switched off the engine and jumped down. 'Afternoon, ladies.' He nodded and walked around to the back of the vehicle.

'This cannot be them,' Valerie whispered. 'We aren't prepared...'

Suddenly Lucy was standing beside them, staring at the trucks and the first man limping down from it. 'That was quick.'

Valerie sprang forward, remembering her duty was as a nurse first and administrator second. Audrey went down one step but then turned back to Lucy. 'Find Owen and Alf, tell them to take all the furniture out of the morning room-' She stopped as Owen and Alf came around the side of the house to help offload the stretchers.

Lucy stared as the gravel drive filled with people. 'But-'

'Tell Cook that we'll need tea and have Betsy ready to wash the floor once the rug has been re-moved and—'

'Enough, go.' Lucy took one look at a man being brought out on a stretcher and then fled back inside to get help.

Audrey quickly forgot about the space shortages and went to aid the drivers. Some of the patients had physical injuries, but many did not. A number of the men could walk into the house. However, their faces wore masks of pain, their eyes vacant and staring. A male voice, not loud but authoritative, reached her, though as yet she couldn't see him. She rounded the first truck and immediately helped a wounded man step down onto the ground. 'Here we are.' She smiled into his pained face. 'Let me help you inside.'

'No, I can make it, help Mick there, he's had a bad trip.' The soldier pointed to another man in the dimness of the truck, before hobbling away to the house.

Audrey peered into the back of the truck at the man sitting hunched over. The bandages on his thigh were blood stained. 'Can you manage to come to the end of the seat?'

He looked up, slowly focusing on her. 'I don't…think so.'

'No bother, I'll come to you.' Audrey heaved herself up into the truck, once more thankful for wearing her overalls, which had become a habit now. 'So, let's be having you out of this old thing and into a nice comfy bed,' she said cheerfully, trying to make the man forget his pain, if only for a minute. 'What's your name?'

'Hughes, Sergeant Hughes.'

'Put your arm around my shoulders then, Sergeant Hughes, that's it, I've got you.'

Somehow, she managed to get him to the end of the bench without either of them falling over, bent as they were.

'Need some help?' Robert stood looking up at them.

'Oh, you're still here. Good. Yes, please.' Between the two of them, they succeeded in getting the injured man down from the truck and into the house, where they deposited him on a chair in the hall.

Confusion and noise now reigned in the serene house, but above it all was a commanding voice that as yet Audrey couldn't put a face to. Officers came down from their rooms to help in any way they could, but with so many people milling about, furniture being carried away, medical supplies brought in and cot beds erected, chaos soon erupted and everything took longer to sort out and organise.

'I say, the fire has gone out in the drawing room.' An older officer stood in the hall, quite unprepared to fix the problem himself, and succeeded to get in everyone's way.

Walking past him into the room with a large box of bandages, Audrey gave him a quelling look over her shoulder. He was the one officer she didn't like amongst those who billeted here to recuperate from their injuries. Audrey felt he was able to return to his regiment now, and that he pretended his chest was worse than it was. He liked the lifestyle of Twelve Pines too much to leave, and elderly Doctor Penshaw humoured him. 'Perhaps you could relight it, Colonel Barnes?'

He looked disgusted, drawing himself up to his full height. 'Now look here, I've never lit a fire in my life!'

Dumping the box on the floor with the others, Audrey raised an eyebrow at him. 'Neither had I until this war started, and soldiers came to live in my home. So, I believe it's time you learnt, sir, as I have done.'

She turned and banged smack into a man's broad chest. 'Oh lord, so sorry.'

'My fault.'

That voice. Distracted, she reached out to steady him, thinking he was a patient, but when she looked up into his face, her hands hovered in mid-air. The bluest eyes, a light penetrating blue, smiled down at her from a handsome, but tired face. Audrey felt something stir in her chest, robbing her of breath and all thought. She wanted to stay right where she was and look at him forever.

He held out his hand. 'Captain Harding, doctor.'

She slid her hand into his and the contact sent shivers up her arm to filter through her whole body. 'Au-Audrey Pearson.'

'Ah, Pearson,' his smiled widened, 'daughter of the house?'

She nodded, not trusting herself to speak coherently to this giant of a man. Although he was tall, it wasn't just the physical size that made him appear large, it was his quiet manner and an aura around him that gave him the appearance of someone great, someone you could trust, someone you would want to have beside you. She didn't understand how she knew all this from simply staring at him, only there was a solid connection she felt with this man and the knowledge of it warmed her soul as nothing had ever done before. Just looking at him made her feel safe, warm, secure.

All at once, her senses became aware again of the surrounding clamour. She stepped back, her cheeks growing hot, and as if he sensed the change too, the smile disappeared to be replaced with a frown. Worry entered his eyes as he tore his gaze from her and swept it around the room. 'I'd best get on with it then.'

Chapter Two

Throughout the evening and well into the night, Twelve Pines was a flurry of activity as Audrey and the nurses settled everyone in. Every room either held beds or boxes of supplies and medical equipment.

Their evening meal was a rushed affair with Mrs Graham, the family's old cook, giving out tea, toast and soup to anyone who walked into the kitchen.

Slowly the house grew quiet, as patients slumbered, exhausted by the eventful day. The new nurses joined the others and went up to their quarters in the attic. Outside, the chirping of crickets serenaded the countryside to sleep.

Audrey found a moment to sit in the kitchen, the warmth from the Aga still cosy. She stirred up the fire enough to boil the kettle. Lucy and their father, Ernest, had long retired. Audrey frowned, thinking of her father. He was becoming weaker, his chest cold adding to his frailness. He'd never been strong, physically, but his presence within the family had never wavered. His family meant everything to him, was all he had lived for, but with his darling wife dying and then the following year war broke out to take his only son, it was all becoming too much. The estate didn't hold his interest. He was never keen on riding the hunt or shooting parties even when they were held before the war and life was happy. She realised he was old, past seventy-five now. He'd married Joanna late, at nearly fifty, while his wife was only a debutant.

Taking the cup and saucer down from the dresser, Audrey smiled. Her mother had told her once that she had loved Ernest Pearson from the moment they met at a ball held in York. She was a social beauty, a prize for any man, and when she had picked *old Ernest,* society had collectively gasped and gossiped about the age difference. Only, Joanna knew her heart and wanted a man who was gentle and caring, someone she could trust to keep her safe. In that, Ernest never failed until the cancer came and won, taking her from them.

The door opened, jolting Audrey out of her reverie. Captain Harding stood poised on the step leading down into the kitchen. Audrey's heart somersaulted at the sight of him. During the evening, as everyone worked, she'd found herself searching for him, listening for his voice. He'd been busy with the patients that came in the trucks, for they were badly injured, still in shock, and in need of his care.

'Sorry to disturb you.' His small, weary smile made her stomach flip. He looked lost, unsure.

She wanted to reach out and bring his head down on her shoulder and hold him there. 'No, you're not disturbing me at all. Please, come and sit down.' Being alone with him made her cheeks flame, and she turned away to get another cup and saucer. 'Have you eaten? I can make you something.'

He stepped down and walked across the stone floor to the table, his size dominating the room. 'I'd really like a cup of tea and perhaps a sandwich?'

She darted him a quick smile, suddenly nervous and self-conscious for the first time in her adult life. 'We don't have much to offer, not like before the war, but I'm sure I can find enough to make a sandwich. Cook tries her bets to keep a good larder despite the rationing…' She went into the larder and found bread, linen wrapped cheese and corned beef on a marble slab.

Returning to the table, she hesitated for a moment, watching him mash the tea in the teapot. His big hands moving deftly, his long fingers tapered with short clean fingernails. 'D-Do you take sugar and milk? We're bound to have a little of both somewhere.'

He looked up. 'No, save the rations. I can have it without.'

'Me too.' Audrey set the food on the table, kept her gaze lowered, and began making him sandwiches. Her body quivered, being so close to him, as though it knew this man. She couldn't understand it. She had been surrounded by many men for the last few years and never considered them possible beaus, and before the war she used to flirt with her brother's friends, but that seemed all so innocent now, when she was a girl. Now though, her body reacted to the physical presence of this man and she didn't know what to do about it.

'You handled today very well. Sister Lewis told me you have never been this full before.' The captain filled the teacups. 'Though I suppose you've become used to the routine by now.'

'In a way, yes, but we've always been a small concern because we are so far from the larger hospitals. Never more than eight men and three nurses at one time, and the soldiers who stayed here, weren't as dreadfully sick as those that came today.' She piled the sandwiches on a plate for him and passed it across.

'The ones that came with me are special cases, mostly shell-shocked. Some of whom have no physical injuries, but their minds have shut down, refusing to cope with what they have seen and done.'

'They will find peace here. At least the most peace to be found in the middle of a war.'

'It's a beautiful home. I'd have liked to have seen it in its former glory.' He took a bite of his sandwich.

'Yes, my mother decorated it wonderfully, but now...' She shrugged. 'We've doubled in the number of soldiers and we weren't even asked if we could accommodate them. My father first proposed to the Army about becoming a convalescence home for a few officers needing a rest. We have the sea air and are in the country, but what we thought might be the odd officer every now and then, has turned into a full-scale operation.'

'It's happening everywhere. However, the men do need somewhere away from the carnage to recuperate. You are doing more help than you know.'

'Well, we shan't complain then.' She smiled.

'There are whispers of an allied invasion being planned soon.' Harding picked up the other half of the sandwich, his blue eyes dull, as though they were seeing beyond the food in his hands to another place. 'They've decided to send as many of the soldiers out of the main hospitals as they can, to country homes and small village hospitals.'

'In readiness for the wounded when they're shipped back across the channel.' She knew the story. 'Will it ever end?'

'Yes, it will, one day. It must. The world can't sustain a large-scale war forever.'

She rose and put away the bread, cheese and corned beef, then came and sat back down. It was nice to have him here. A strong able-bodied man, an intelligent man to talk to. Father would like him. She sipped her tea, watching him eat. Stubble shadowed his square jawline, and she noticed a small white scar under his ear. 'Will you be here for long, Captain Harding?'

He swallowed a mouthful of sandwich. 'Yes, I think so.'

Her stomached clenched at the thought of having this man in her home for months. She liked him very much and wanted to know everything about him. 'Why haven't they sent you to the field hospitals in France?'

Harding drank more of his tea, not looking at her, and then stood. 'Thank you for the meal. I should be checking the patients again.'

Audrey stood also. 'Yes, of course.' She collected his plate and teacup. 'Can you find your way around?'

He stopped by the door. 'Yes, thank you.'

She didn't want him to go, and she didn't understand his abruptness. Had she been too forward, too nosy? 'If you need anything during the night, I'm upstairs, second door on the right.'

'Sister Lewis is doing the night shift, I'm sure the two of us will cope.' He opened the door and gave her a lingering look before walking out.

The room seemed suddenly chilly. Audrey hugged herself and it had nothing to do with the cold. He'd put her in her place. His whole manner said don't come too close or ask any questions that aren't your business. Well, she'd listen to his unspoken rule. He was a doctor in her home to care for wounded men. One day he would leave and return to his home wherever that was.

Then it struck her. Could he be married? Her skin goose-bumped, but at the same time her cheeks grew red with embarrassment. Lord, did he think she'd fallen for him? Had she? No, of course she hadn't. She'd only spoken to him twice, met him just today. She shook herself. *You're being ridiculous.*

After checking the fire was banked down for the night and everything was clean and tidy for Mrs Graham in the morning, Audrey left the kitchen and went along the corridor. If her footstep paused outside of the morning room, where she knew Captain Harding was sitting with his patients, she didn't stop to think about it.

~ ~ ~

Audrey rounded the side of the house pushing the wheelbarrow full of horse manure. Along the house wall grew the last of her mother's favourite white and yellow roses. The family had been adamant that this rose bed wouldn't be sacrificed for vegetables.

She took her garden fork off the pile and began forking out the manure around the roses. The warm day heralded spring and the coming summer. Birds chattered in the birch trees behind her and she caught a glimpse of a grey squirrel darting through the long grass around the trunks. The roses, their new leaves bright green, had some early buds and Audrey paused to touch them gently. Her mother spent hours in the garden, both Owen and Alf adored her and nothing she asked was too much for them to do. If she wanted a pond, they dug it, if she wanted a yew hedge, they planted it. Audrey wondered if they would one day think of her in the same way. In a lot of ways, she had taken her mother's role in the house, but the war had changed so much. All of the younger staff gone, leaving her to do their work. There weren't enough hours in the day to get it all done. She'd have to make Lucy help more. Only, she tried to shield Lucy from the hard work as much as possible. Still, Lucy was no longer a baby, even if everyone still thought of her as so. If only the war hadn't started, they'd still have Robbie with them, and staff, and even without their mother, life would have been much the same as before.

From an open window above, soft music flowed out from a radio. Humming along with it, she worked her way down the front of the bed, turning the manure into the rich soil. Movement to the side caught her attention and she paused her digging. Captain Harding, and three of the men that arrived at Twelve Pines with him, strolled across the lawns. They low conversation didn't reach her, but each man looked sad and vulnerable. Next to the strand of birch trees, the lawn widened again, sloping a little towards the carp pond with its angel fountain. The small group sat or laid around the pond. Captain Harding hunkered down, talking to them, some nodded while one man, Nielson, stared away over the fields that led to the cliffs.

Not wanting to be caught watching them, especially by the Captain, Audrey continued forking the soil. However, thoughts of the Captain lingered in her mind. It seemed as though all her senses where attuned to him and she wasn't sure what to do about it. They lived in the same house, ate at the same table, used the same rooms. The times she enjoyed with Valerie were now restricted because he shared the nurses' office. She could no longer grab a cup of tea with Valerie and perch on the end of Val's desk to discuss movies, books or music, or to simply have a moan and a light-hearted gossip. Everywhere she turned, Captain Harding's presence loomed large. The nurses near swooned whenever he walked by and old Mrs Graham cooked her fingers to the bone trying to create tasty things for the *'good doctor'*.

'You seem busy.'

'Oh!' Audrey jumped at the sound of the Captain's voice behind her.

Instantly he put out his hand, his expression full of apology. 'I'm so sorry, I didn't mean to startle you.'

'No, it's fine.' She blushed furiously; her cheeks hot. 'I-I was miles away.'

'You must enjoy gardening then, for it to soothe you so.' The men were no longer with him and she noticed them sauntering towards the tennis court.

'Yes, I do enjoy it. My mother was the same and I never understood how she could devote so much time to it, but now I do. It's soothing.'

His blue eyes softened. 'We all need something that relaxes us. Though sometimes you seem to work too hard, or at least it looks that way to me.'

'There are some jobs I would prefer not doing, but this isn't one of them. Cleaning up after the chimney sweep is a chore I detest.' She laughed and brushed a wayward curl back behind her ear. She looked down at her old overalls and for once wished she didn't wear them. She should get Lucy to paint her nails, too and—

'I'm surprised this bed isn't growing vegetables like the others.'

'We refused to give this one up. Father said he'd rather see all the lawns ploughed over before giving up Mother's last roses.'

'Sensible. The war mustn't take everything, must it?' He smiled.

She returned his smile, inside she felt warm. When he was near, she believed magic happened within her. Her body grew languid yet strung tight at the same time. There was no understanding of it. Only, she knew that since his arrival, her life had turned topsy-turvy. New feelings, emotions and sensations over-whelmed her in his presence.

'I suggested to the men that a game of tennis might be in order. Are there racquets and balls around?'

'Yes indeed.' She pointed to the small shed behind the court. 'All that they need is in there. The lock might be rusty after winter. Alf will have some oil, see him to fix it or I can find him for you.'

'We'll manage. We're not little boys.' He winked.

'The court might not be in the best shape.' She placed the fork in the wheelbarrow, eager to help. 'I'll find a broom and sweep it.'

'No.' He touched her arm when she went to move away. 'We are grown men and can actually use a broom.' He grinned.

Her heart seemed to sigh at his closeness. 'I don't mind, really.'

'You have enough to do. Besides, the men need to do something, it helps their recovery. That's why I suggested tennis for those fit enough to play. Sitting around all day gives them time to dwell and they don't need to dwell too much.'

'I've noticed a vast improvement to many of the new arrivals. You must be happy with the results so far?'

He looked back to where the men were inspecting the court. 'A lot of their recovery is due to the fact they are away from the front line. Sometimes the mind just needs time to relax. Here, where the threat of being killed or the need to kill another is vastly reduced and so they can return, somewhat, back to the men they were before the war changed them.'

'But they have to go back eventually, don't they?' she murmured.

'Some will, yes, those that have come here for a respite and are not mentally damaged will definitely return. The worst cases, and thankfully we only have one or two of those, will never go near a battlefield again.'

'I wish they could all come home,' she whispered.

The music above was interrupted by a news bulletin and Captain Harding stepped back. 'I'd better get this game sorted.'

'Well, while you do that, how about I arrange for some drinks to be brought down?'

'There's no need.' He straightened; his expression serious. 'We'll manage.'

'No, I want to. I could even be the scorer if you would like?'

He frowned. 'What about your gardening?'

'I'm nearly finished here.'

Stepping back more, he nodded, but didn't look enthusiastic. 'Perhaps your sister could be persuaded to join us too, or some of the nurses?'

'Yes, I'll ask.'

'Good.' He turned and walked away. Audrey had the impression he didn't really want her joining in the game. Had she overstepped the mark again?

Chapter Three

'And here I thought summer was on its way.' Valerie chuckled, as she added another log to the kitchen fire. They were sitting at the far end of the kitchen, a place originally used by the staff to dine, but was now the area for the family and Valerie, who'd become family, to use. Their removal to the kitchen left the drawing room for the men to use without feeling self-conscious in front of the family. The small fireplace kept the room warm when in use along with the Aga at the other end of the long room.

Audrey glanced up from reading her book. 'I know. I had cleaned out that fireplace, thinking we wouldn't need it again until the end of September.'

Valerie sat back at the square table and picked up her knitting. 'It wouldn't be so bad if we didn't have that cold wind.'

'Could we have some tea, Audrey dear?' Her father asked, from behind his newspaper.

'Yes, of course, but Mrs Graham mentioned we need more tea though, so it will have to be a weak pot.' She frowned. 'Our rations aren't stretching with the extra men.'

Her father lowered the newspaper, his face a mask of guilt. 'Oh my.'

'What?'

'I totally forgot. I do apologise.'

'Forgot what?' Audrey closed her book and rose.

'In my post I received the extra ration coupons needed. It slipped my mind. You know what I'm like with correspondence. I hate it.'

Audrey bent over and kissed the top of his head. 'It's fine Father, I'll see to it, and Mrs Graham will be most happy when I tell her in the morning.'

'Very good, my dear. It does tend to gather into the most enormous piles on my desk.' Her father sagged in the deep chair, his favourite one brought in from the drawing room.

'You should get Lucy to answer your correspondence for you.'

'Where is Lucy?'

'At the Red Cross meeting in Bridlington.' Audrey went and stoked up the Aga and then filled the kettle with water.

'She's a good girl.' Her father murmured.

Audrey remained silent but sent Valerie a telling look. They both knew it was doubtful that Lucy attended any such meeting and instead would go dancing or to the pictures with her friends. She had secretly asked both Audrey and Valerie to lend her some money as she'd already spent her allowance, and you didn't need money at a Red Cross meeting.

'Go ask Captain Harding if he wishes to join us, Audrey.' Her father spoke again from behind his newspaper. 'The man works too hard. When I get up in the night, I see his lamp on late nearly every time. Once it was still on at two in the morning.'

'Yes, he reads or writes notes until late.' Val agreed. 'I don't think he needs a lot of sleep. Also, poor Nielson's is not doing well.'

Audrey set out the tray with cups and saucers. 'Nielson's nightmares are terrifying. His screams are so piercing, so agonising, the poor man.'

Her father flicked his paper straight. 'Go find the Captain, Audrey. Get him to come and share a brew with us and rest for a minute or two. We have to make him feel at ease here. He must be made to feel this will be his home now, not just a place to work.'

Valerie patted his hand. 'Like you did with me.'

Ernest smiled fondly. 'Indeed, another daughter I have in you, Val.'

Taking a deep breath, Audrey left the kitchen and went in search of the doctor who was everyone's favourite, but who remained something of an enigma to them all, especially to her. She wished it wasn't so.

She looked in the office and the drawing room, here, stopping to chat with the few officers playing cards, before going upstairs to the bedrooms. Robbie's room now held three beds in it and there she found Harding sitting on a chair, the lamp lit, reading softly to Sergeant Hughes. The sergeant was sound asleep; little snores erupted with each intake of breath.

The scene touched her. Captain Harding's quiet presence easily comforted the most unsettled person. She only wished he had the same effect on her, instead it was opposite. Being near him set her stomach fluttering and her mind spinning for reason.

Harding glanced up as she entered. 'Miss Pearson. Is something wrong?' he whispered, closing the book. It was one of Robbie's old books by Daniel Defoe, *A General History of the Pyrates*.

'Not at all, Captain,' she whispered back. 'My father just wanted to know if you'd like to come down to the kitchen and have some tea with us, that's all.'

He indicated for her to leave the room with him and in the hallway, he turned and gently closed the bedroom door. 'Thank you, but I'll have to refuse your father's offer. I'll be making my last round shortly and then I've notes to write up.'

'You couldn't spare a couple of minutes? It won't take long.'

'No, not really.'

'There's some of Mrs Graham's currant cake, too.' She tried not to sound desperate for his company, but she realised she very much wanted him to spend time with her, on any pretence. It was a taunt having him in the house, but not being able to spend time getting to truly know him.

He gazed down at her and she shivered slightly at his scrutiny. Why did he sometimes look at her with near hatred in his eyes? Then, at other times, his eyes softened, their colour changing, and her body would respond in answer to some unknown question.

'Sorry, not tonight, another time. Thank your father for the offer for me please.' He hesitated a moment more before leaving to enter another bedroom.

~ ~ ~

'Can we go for a walk down to the beach?' Lucy asked, flipping the bed sheet up and then pulling it down tight.

Audrey put a pillow in its case and sighed. 'I don't know if I can today. Val is having problems with one of the nurses, and—'

'They aren't your responsibility. You do enough, we *all* do enough! Blasted army, blasted *war*.' Lucy gave the sheet a vicious tug. 'I'm so tired of it. I want some fun.'

'Lucy—'

'Oh, I just remembered. I forgot to tell you yesterday that there's a dance on in Brid this Saturday. Please come with me.'

'We don't have enough petrol rations to get to Fraisthorpe, never mind Bridlington.'

Lucy grinned. 'All sorted. Owen said he'll drive us in the old cart.'

'The farm cart?' Audrey laughed. 'You'll not be fit to be seen after travelling in a cart.'

'We'll sweep it out and put blankets in.' Shrugging, Lucy placed the thin green blanket on the end of the bed. 'Do say yes, Aud. I'm desperate for a dance. You adore jitterbugging and you're so good at it. I do hope there'll be a few Americans in town, they dance so much better than English men.'

'Any man is preferable rather than dancing with other woman, as we've done before.'

'Yes, but that was over a year ago. Now we have so many soldiers based in this area. I heard the Scottish lancers are in town or coming or something.' Lucy spun around. 'Men everywhere. I can't wait.'

'Well, I'll see. If Valerie doesn't need me, perhaps.'

Lucy squealed and jumped over the bed to hug and kiss her. A discreet cough separated them, and they turned to find Captain Harding lounging in the doorway, smiling at them in his quiet manner. Audrey's heart did a spin, as it always did whenever she heard or saw him. In the last week, she'd made sure never to be alone with the doctor, not wanting to give him the slightest reason to even think she saw him as anything other than an army doctor here to do a job.

She forced herself to act normal, sophisticated. 'Captain Harding, can we be of help?'

His blue eyes held hers for a fraction longer before he straightened. 'Yes, Miss Pearson. Sister Lewis was looking for you, as we believe we need another room for Lieutenant Nielson. Unfortunately, his nightmares are keeping the rest of the men in his room awake. Is it possible to prepare another room?'

Audrey frowned, she too had heard the poor solider screaming at night, his cries for them to take cover echoed around the house. 'Certainly, Captain Harding. However, my Father believes the rear parlour has some damp, perhaps there's a leak in the roof, we need to fix that before the room is used again.'

'I see.' He rubbed his chin, frowning. 'I'd prefer to keep Nielson in his room, as he's familiar with it, and move the other two men out.'

'We could use Sister Lewis' office and move everything in there into the drawing room. The office isn't large, but it'll fit two beds in it.'

'But the officers use the drawing room, Audrey.' Lucy said.

'The officers will simply have to use the dining room and conservatory for their recreational pursuits.' Audrey stepped towards the door.

'Yes, I agree. Sounds like an excellent plan.' Captain Harding didn't move to let her pass and she stopped to stare at him. 'I was wondering Miss Pearson…'

Her mouth dried. 'Yes?'

'I overheard you and your sister,' he shot a look at Lucy, 'about your impending dance and I was wondering-'

'Do you wish to go with us, Captain?' Lucy asked, her eyes bright. 'And dance the jitterbug with Audrey? She's ever so good.'

Audrey swallowed, knowing her cheeks flamed. A night of dancing with the handsome Captain? She felt light-headed at the thought.

He laughed softly. 'I'm afraid not, Miss Pearson, but I do think it would be beneficial for some of the patients, if they could accompany you? A few of them are in desperate need of some semblance of normality. It helps their healing to remember and experience activities that are good fun and have no connection to war and death...'

'Oh yes!' Lucy clapped. 'We never get enough men at these dances. Most of the time we have to dance with other women. What a brilliant idea, Captain.'

'Are-are they well enough to attend?' Audrey murmured, continually saddened by the fine men who were staying at Twelve Pines. They suffered such misery. A couple of officers, Johnson and Price, had changed dramatically since arriving and would happily chat and help around the house. There were others though that still kept apart and quiet, refusing to discuss what they'd experienced.

'I would say three or four of them, yes. Not the men who arrived with me, obviously, but the others are ready for a little light entertainment. It'll do them good before they return to the front.'

'They leave soon?' For some reason she couldn't look at him, frightened, she supposed. Frightened he would see something in her face, the emotion she felt

36

being near him. What a shame the good-looking doctor wasn't coming with them. She could smell the subtle shaving cologne he wore, a mixture of sandalwood and something else she couldn't name.

'Yes. Jamieson, Winthrop, Fielding and Battersby all leave a week on Friday. They've passed their assessments.'

She nodded and took a step, wanting to be gone from the room, from him and from the emotions warring in her. 'I'll go find Sister Lewis.'

'Miss Pearson?'

Side-by-side in the doorway they faced each other. Audrey's head only reached his shoulder. She stared at the shining buttons on his uniform, not trusting herself to look up at him. 'Yes, Captain?'

'On second thoughts, I think I might accompany the men to the dance.'

She glanced at him, her eyes wide and the difficulty to swallow occurred again. 'Very well…'

'Just in case the men need me, of course,' he whispered.

Audrey's skin tingled as though he had caressed her. 'Of course…'

~ ~ ~

Lucy preened in front of the mirror. 'Do I look all right?'

'I've told you so, a dozen times already.' Audrey, sitting on the end of her bed, rolled her eyes as she struggled to buckle her black shoes.

'I hope there are more soldiers this time. Though it's good of Captain Harding to allow some of our officers to attend.'

'Well, they have nearly recovered. Any physical injuries they had have healed and apparently a night of mixing with good people will help their mental state too.'

Lucy dabbed on more lipstick. 'Is it true that Captain Harding is a doctor of the mind as well as a normal doctor?'

'Yes…' Audrey's fingers stilled on the stiff buckle. Valerie had informed her last night while they shared a cup of hot chocolate in the kitchen that Captain Jake Harding was interested in the men's minds after they'd been in battle – a psychiatry doctor. This news worried Audrey. Would he study her mannerisms, her actions when she was near? She had to try even harder now not to be noticed by him. Her embarrassment would be complete if he realised she was in awe of him.

'So, are the men we have all mad?' Lucy pouted at her reflection.

'No, not mad, but…damaged a little.' Audrey shook her head, mentally wiping the captain from her thoughts. 'They've seen things, horrible things, and they need someone to talk to about it, to help them understand it in their minds.'

'Will we get more of them?' Lucy's hand hesitated in mid-air. 'More mad soldiers from the front, like that patient who screams every night?'

'He's not mad, Lucy,' Audrey defended, finally getting the buckle done. 'He's in shock from being buried beneath mud when a bomb landed close to him in a dugout. I won't have you saying our poor men here are mad.'

'Then why do we have a doctor that treats the insane?'

Audrey glared at her sister and felt like swearing a word she'd heard the men say when they were in pain. 'He doesn't treat the insane. Don't start gossip.

Captain Harding helps the men understand what's happened to them. The men need to be well in body and mind before they are subjected again to the hell that's in France!'

'All right!' Lucy held her hands up as if in surrender. 'I was only asking.'

'Well, just show some respect. Remember Robbie.'

At the mention of their darling brother, lost in some foreign battle, buried in a foreign grave, Lucy nodded. 'I'm sorry.'

Audrey smiled lovingly, forgetting how young and sheltered her sister was sometimes. 'I know. It's fine.'

A cheeky grin replaced Lucy's sad expression. 'Is the good doctor married?'

'How would I know?' Audrey fiddled with the buttons at the front of her dress.

'You know more about him than I do.'

'Scarcely.'

'He gives you looks.'

Audrey's head snapped up. 'What looks? What do you mean?'

Laughing, Lucy touched perfume at her wrists and behind her ears. 'He watches you when he thinks no one is looking.'

'Nonsense.' Although she denied it, Audrey secretly hoped it was true. Her stomach fluttered like moths around a lamp.

'It's true, but I bet he can't say anything to you because he has a wife.' Lucy adjusted the red bow in her hair. 'I bet he has a cripple wife, who's bedridden and frail with-'

'Stop it!'

'You should see your face.' Lucy bent over laughing, holding her side.

Audrey looked around for something to throw at her sister.

A knock on the bedroom door preceded their father. He stood there, smiling at them. 'I can hear you both from the landing. Now, don't you both look lovely.'

'Thank you, Father.' Audrey rose and smoothed down the dusky pink silk dress she wore, fashioned from a former ball gown of her mother's that she and Lucy had found in the storage trunks. After a night of alterations, they'd managed to make the dress closely resemble the latest style.

'Is the cart ready, Father?' Lucy placed her red shawl around her shoulders, letting it drop low. 'It is cold out?'

'The evening appears pleasant. A full moon and not too cool.' Their father pulled Lucy's shawl up more around her neck, for her red polka-dot dress had a low neckline, which he frowned at. 'Owen has the cart out the front, and yes, the weather is nice now, but have you got a coat for later tonight?'

Lucy kissed him loudly, leaving red lipstick on his cheek. 'We'll be grand, Father, don't worry.' She flounced out of the room.

Audrey smiled at her antics and kissed her father more chastely. 'I'll keep an eye on her.'

'Yes, do, especially with if there are Americans about. You know how silly she gets.' He patted her arm, his lined face relaxing slightly. 'Shall I wait up?'

'No, we could be late.'

'Be careful.'

'Always.' She kissed him again and went downstairs where Captain Harding and Valerie were talking to the officers going to the dance. The men wore full dress uniform and looked distinguished and happy to be away from sickness and memories, if only for one night.

Valerie looked up as Audrey descended. 'Oh, you do look splendid, Audrey.'

Captain Harding turned and stared at her, his blue eyes narrowing before he quickly walked out the front door.

Audrey faltered on the last step, absurdly hurt by his behaviour. However, she was soon swept up into the men's jollity, as they all begged dances with her and Lucy while they hoisted themselves up onto the back of the cart. Yet, her smiles and laughter were strained, for Captain Harding's actions lingered in her mind. He ran hot and cold with her, making her doubt herself, and feel self-conscious – things she'd rarely felt before he arrived.

As Owen slapped the reins for the draught horse to move on down the drive and onto Pearson's lane, the officers, Jamieson, Edwards, Winthrop and Fielding declared they were escorting the two prettiest girls in Bridlington. Lucy basked in their appraisal, but Audrey only smiled and stared at the back of Captain Harding who sat up the front beside Owen. She didn't enjoy the confusion of her feelings where he was concerned, and neither did she like the amount of time she spent thinking about him. What good did it do? She could count on one hand how many times he raised a smile in her direction and when he did, he seemed to immediately regret it. Did he watch her, like Lucy said? Could they become friends? She shivered, silently praying it would be so.

'That's a lovely sunset, Miss Pearson,' Fielding leaned close to whisper.

Audrey looked towards the west, the orange sun setting behind the distant ranges beyond Carnaby

Moor, casting a pinky-rose glow over the land. 'Yes, it is.' She smiled. She turned the other way, letting the sea breeze lift her hair. 'That's Fraisthorpe Sands down there, they lead on to the South Sands.' She pointed between the trees to the cliffs. 'You should have a walk along the beach.'

Fielding smiled, his grey eyes crinkling behind his glasses. The road dipped and below them the ocean shimmered gold of the late sunset. 'I just might do that.'

'Though mind the barbed wire.' She winked. When she glanced away again, she realised Captain Harding had twisted in the seat to talk to Captain Jamieson, but his gaze had drifted to her.

Reliving his earlier snub, she lifted her chin and turned away, closing her eyes against the salty breeze. Let him have some of his own medicine.

Before long they were trundling along the streets of Bridlington. They passed the Roxy theatre and bowled along to the small hall tucked down a lane behind a church.

'I do hope the RAF from Carnaby are here.' Lucy glowed with good health and youth. She dazzled the officers with her friendly smile and open affection. Tucking her hands through the arms of Jamieson and Winthrop, she led the party to the hall.

Blackout meant there were no coloured lanterns strung out to welcome guests, but inside, the hall was well decorated with paper chains and bright lights which changed colours, flashing glittery shades across the walls. The band were at the end of the hall set up on the stage.

Audrey stood and gazed about. She hadn't been to a dance for many months and had missed the vibrant noisiness, the fun, and the freedom of letting the music be everything to you for a few hours. As the band struck up, and Officer Fielding took her hand, Audrey forgot the demands of looking after the house and land, forgot the shortages, the frustrations of having her home run by the army, by the war, and simply let Fielding twirl her around and around. For a while she looked for Captain Harding, watching to see who he danced with, but he took no partners to the dance floor and instead stared at her for a short time before disappearing.

The music grew faster, the crowd swelled and Audrey, pushing Harding from her mind, lost her inhibitions and let Fielding, who was surprisingly a good dancer, guide her through dance steps and routines they both knew by heart.

After the dance finished, she did a waltz with Winthrop, then a foxtrot with Jamieson before another waltz with Fielding. Everywhere there were men and women in uniform. Audrey spotted Lucy chuckling with two RAF men and then the next time she saw her, she was dancing with a spotty youth, who kept treading on her toes.

The dancing was kept formal due to the number of older couples, but after the interval most went gone home, leaving the younger ones to dance the night away. Audrey, never short of partners, tangoed, jitterbugged with an American air force pilot from Chicago, and jived until her feet hurt.

Too soon, the evening was drawing to a close. The hall had become uncomfortably warm, but the atmosphere was still electric, those brave men and women who'd be returning to the war again tomorrow were laughing, singing and dancing, not wanting the night to end.

Audrey went to the refreshments table and drank a glass of water then stood at the edge of the dance floor to regain her breath. The coloured lights dimmed, and the mood changed as the slower dances replaced the high energy ones. Surreptitiously, people were pairing off, the music became softer.

The last dance was announced and, as always, Audrey felt a sense of loss. She hated the last dance, of saying goodbye to the fun and light-heartedness. She never promised anyone the last dance, preferring to use it as a good excuse to grab her things and go before the crowd dispersed. Turning away, she bumped into a uniformed man.

'You make a habit of turning blind and bumping into me, Miss Pearson.' Captain Harding smiled down.

Her legs seemed to lose all ability to hold her upright. 'I do apologise, Captain, I was wanting to find my sister.' She chanced a glance at him, and his blue eyes held hers. 'It-It's time to go.'

'Not yet, the last dance is about to begin. Your sister is dancing with Winthrop.' He held out his hand. 'May I?'

That simple gesture nearly brought her to her knees. Wordlessly, mindlessly, she laid her hand in his and let him guide her to the middle of the floor as the lights dimmed even more, giving the couples a sense of privacy and seclusion.

As the music began, he gathered her closer. Audrey thought her heart would stop beating. Couples packed the floor, their last chance of a dance, and so they had little room to move in. The Captain kept a firm hold of her and she let out a pent-up breath as they swayed to the music. The touch of his hand in hers, the feel of his uniform jacket beneath her fingers made her dreamy. The muted light, the soft soulful music and the handsomest man in the room holding her created an impenetrable aura around her. She felt invincible, beautiful, special.

She closed her eyes, breathing in his scent, feeling his fingers on her lower back. If she turned her head just the slightest, she could easily kiss his neck, her heeled evening shoes gave her a little more height to do so. His thigh brushed hers as they swayed, and Audrey's insides melted into a pool of sensations and longing. Did he sense her ache, her confusion of wanting him so much that it wiped out all other thought?

All too soon the music stopped, the blare of the lights blinded them as they were switched back on. Blinking, Audrey smiled in the garish brightness. 'Thank you, Captain Harding. It was-'

'It was a pleasure, Miss Pearson.' He dropped her hand and stepped back, once more wearing his cool expression. With a nod, he spun on his heel and marched across the emptying dance floor.

Alone, Audrey glanced down her shoes, trying to swallow the knot of emotion clogging her throat at his abrupt exit. She felt crushed. All her longing disappeared into a ball of embarrassing rejection that twisted her stomach. She'd been such a fool – again!

'Audrey!' Lucy came running to her side, out of breath. She grabbed Audrey's arm and they walked to the closet room to find their shawls. 'Wasn't it a great night? One of the best for certain. I've never danced so much in my life. Did you enjoy it? Who did you dance with? I met a wonderful American. He's called Russ. What a name. Russ. It's so American. He's from Detroit…'

Thankful that Lucy didn't need any input from her for the conversation, Audrey let her prattle on as they went outside to the cart.

All the way home the officers and Lucy laughed, sang and talked until they were hoarse while Audrey sat huddled with a blanket around her, staring out at the moonlit ocean, wondering if she could ever look at Captain Harding again and be indifferent to him. Only, she knew it wasn't possible. She knew she had fallen in love with a man who was barely polite to her.

Chapter Four

Audrey dragged a bag of seed potatoes out from the rest of the stack in the corner of the barn and tipped them out to inspect for rot. 'What do you think, Owen?'

'They're fine, Miss.' He waved at them with his pipe and tucked his thump into the top of his trousers. 'Alf and I will get them planted this week now the tractors fixed. Though I've spoken to your father and said that if it breaks down *again*, then we'll go back to horse and plough all the time. I've no time for that wretched machine. I could have half a paddock ploughed with old Sugar by the time it takes to mess about with that tractor. Useless it is.'

'We need a new one, that's all.'

'Well, we don't need a new horse, that's for sure. She'll do the job just as well.'

Audrey smiled at him. He was such a traditionalist. 'I'll help when you're ready.'

He scratched his greying whiskers. 'Aye, we'll call if we need you.'

She quirked an eyebrow at him. 'You never call me. For the last four years you've had plenty to say about me working, but I have to do it. It's important to me.'

'Aye, well, you've enough to do in the house without the extra outside work.'

'Valerie, the nurses and Mrs Graham see to everything in the house.'

'Now, Miss, I've told you before, and I'll tell you again, I don't like you out in the fields, it's not right.'

'You and Alf can't do it alone. You two aren't young anymore. We all have to do our share.'

He bristled and puffed out his wide chest. 'It's fine, Miss. We can manage without you. I'll get young Tommy Holmes in to give a hand.'

She nodded, knowing that he liked to protect her as much as he could from the strenuous labour, and started to put the potatoes back into the sack. 'Keep an eye on Tommy. Last time I talked to him, he was speaking of joining up, lying about his age to do so.'

'Nay, he's only fourteen.' Owen sucked on his pipe stem. 'He doesn't look old enough to tie his shoelaces, never mind carry a gun.'

'Yet, they've taken so many boys already, and turned a blind eye to their unshaven faces.'

'True.' He scowled and waved his pipe at her. 'Don't worry about Tommy though. I promised his mother I'd keep him so busy this summer, he'd have no energy to think doing 'owt but sleep when he got home.'

'Audrey?' Valerie's voice echoed through the barn. They turned to see Valerie walking down between the horse stalls.

'I'm here.' Audrey straightened and wiped her hands on her overalls. 'Is something wrong?'

48

'I need you for a moment if that's convenient?' Valerie looked pale; shadows hugged under her eyes.

'Of course.' Once outside, Audrey studied her friend. 'You look tired. Are you sleeping enough? I thought it was your day off. Weren't you going into Bridlington to watch a film?'

Sighing, Val nodded and tucked her hands into the pockets of her navy wool cardigan as they crossed the stable yard. 'I'll go in later. Maybe you'll join me?'

'That'd be nice.' Audrey smiled, but narrowed her eyes to peer Val again. 'You're not getting enough rest. We can't have you becoming ill. Give the other nurses more responsibility.'

'They're too naïve. The new ones are barely eighteen I'm sure.' Valerie stopped and gazed out over the fields beyond the garden. 'I'd like to walk along the beach. We haven't done that together since last summer.'

'Then let us go now.'

'I can't.' Valerie looked at her. 'Nurse Peters is waiting in the office. I summoned her there and I need you and Captain Harding present. That's why I came to find you.'

Audrey ignored her skipping heartbeat at the mention of the doctor and kept walking around to the front of the house. 'Why do you need me?'

'Peters is pregnant and must leave.'

'Lord.' She blinked in surprise. 'Are you sure? Is she sure?'

Valerie paused by the front door. 'Apparently, she's four months gone.'

'Is she the new nurse, the one who has the sniffles all the time?'

'Yes, her continual crying became an issue with the other nurses, and they got the truth from her.'

'I'm guessing she's not married.'

'No.'

Audrey winced. 'Silly girl.'

'Indeed.' Valerie face pinched as though in pain. 'It's not entirely her fault though. The other party should be made accountable.' She took a deep breath. 'But they often get away without a moment's worry. It's not fair. A moment's pleasure can leave lasting hurt.'

Audrey stared at Val's distant look and lightly touched her arm. A light sea breeze lifted their hair. 'Val?'

'Oh, ignore me.' Valerie shook her head. 'Come, let us get it over with.'

Inside the office, Nurse Peters stood by the door, looking ill and condemned. Captain Harding entered after Valerie had sat behind the desk and Audrey leant against the wall by the window. He didn't look Audrey's way, his bearing stiff and business-like. Well, two could play that game.

'Thank you for joining us, Captain.' Valerie glanced from him to Peters. 'As you know, Peters, a nurse in your condition can no longer perform your duties. You will have to return home. Captain Harding and I will take care of all the paperwork concerning your departure.'

'Yes, Sister Lewis.' Peters swayed slightly.

Harding cleared his throat. 'The man responsible, are you still in contact with him?'

Peters' bottom lip quivered. 'No, sir.'

'You are aware of your folly, I'm sure.' Harding's expression tightened.

Audrey groaned. What a stupid question. She scowled at him just as he flicked a look in her direction.

'You have something to say, Miss Pearson?' he asked, with a raise of an eyebrow.

'Not really, Captain, only that I would think Nurse Peters is extremely aware of her mistake. It is changing her life, *will* change her life.'

'Motherhood is no easy matter and being alone and unmarried is a further complication.'

'She may have an understanding family.' Audrey's temper rose at his unyielding manner. What would he know of it anyway? When were men ever victimised about anything?

Nurse Peters covered her face with her hands and sobbed.

Valerie, frowning at the two of them, went to comfort her. 'Come Nurse, shall we take a walk and then I'll help you pack.'

Audrey went to follow them out, but the Captain caught her arm and held her back. 'Tea and sympathy won't help that girl.'

She stared at him, fighting her sexual awareness of him with anger. 'And harsh words will?'

'It may stop her from doing it again.'

'Nothing is so simple.'

'And you would know?' he scoffed. 'A wealthy man's sheltered daughter brought up without ever having seen the darker side of life.'

She yanked her arm out of his grasp. 'You know nothing about me.'

'And you know nothing about life, so don't give out advice on things you know little about!'

'How dare you speak to me like that?' She gave him a look of loathing, but inside she felt sick. Her thoughts concerning him were turning to dust. She'd been badly mistaken to think he could be a man worth loving.

Suddenly, the air raid siren sounded from the nearby village. Valerie stuck her head around the door. 'Come on.'

Audrey dashed out of the room, grateful to be away from Captain Harding before she humiliated herself with silly tears. Why were her emotions so mixed-up lately?

The nurses helped the officers down into the cellar, three of the new patients too ill to leave their beds unaided, were moved on stretchers, but most of the soldiers were now physically able to walk down the cellar steps and sit with everyone else.

Out in the garden, an Anderson air raid shelter had been built for the outside staff if they couldn't make it to the house in time. Audrey often hoped she would never need to use it, as confined spaces made her panic. At least in the large cellar under the house, she didn't have this fear, as the cellar easily accommodated not only wood and coal but also all the wine racks, the cider press and numerous other equipment.

After four years of war and air raids, the cellar had become a comfortable room, with beds and mattresses, pillows and blankets. Mrs Graham had set up a temporary kitchen in one of the alcoves and they'd brought down packs of cards, dominoes and books.

Now, sitting with the others and hearing the faint sound of planes flying over, Audrey looked around at the strained faces in the dim light. Her father sat beside Lucy, holding her hand, his newspaper tucked under his arm. One or two of the nurses were making the men comfortable, talking quietly.

The drone of the planes continued. Each time planes flew overhead, Audrey waited for the whistle of the bombs dropping, wondering if they'd be hit. Luckily, the closest a bomb had come to Twelve

Pines was in 'forty-one, when one landed in the field behind the stables.

The cellar door opened, and they all looked up to see Captain Harding helping Sergeant Hughes gingerly hop down the steps. The doctor's gaze swept around the room, as though looking for someone, then he found Audrey and for a moment they simply looked at each other. The ugly words between them lingered, but she couldn't deny the way her body reacted whenever he was nearby.

He ushered Hughes to a bench seat opposite Audrey and then straightened and gazed down at her. 'Will you help me hand cups of tea around?'

Startled by the request, Audrey nodded automatically.

They edged their way to the far corner of the cellar where Mrs Graham had a hot water urn and tea things. She smiled at them as she set out the trays. 'I've got current cake too.' She cut thin slices and placed them on the edge of the saucers.

Audrey and the Captain moved off with their trays, handing out the tea to everyone. When they finished and met up back at the table, Mrs Graham was talking to Lucy and Ernest.

'I'm sorry,' Harding whispered, not looking at Audrey. 'I never meant to raise my voice in the office. I shouldn't have acted so unprofessionally.' He turned and gave her a small smile. His eyes softened, speaking an apology of their own. 'Can you forgive me?'

'I believe we are all allowed to have an opinion, Captain,' she murmured, wishing her pulse wouldn't race like it did.

'But sometimes people should keep their opinions to themselves.' The smile disappeared and he bent his head. As big and as mature as he was, he still managed to appear like a little boy lost.

Audrey lost her anger and reached out to touch his arm. There was something about this man she didn't understand, but he was deeply unhappy, she sensed it. Could she make him happy, if only for a little while? She touched his hand where it rested on the tray. He looked down at their combined hands. She felt the connection between them and welcomed it, savouring the tingle it brought to her skin. 'Would you like to go for a walk along the beach later?'

He raised his head, his eyes narrowing, searching for some other meaning. A muscle ticked along his jaw. 'Why?'

'Why?' She shrugged and grinned. 'Because we can. Because it's a nice walk. So, would you like me to take you on a tour of our own private beach?'

'Do you think it wise?'

Audrey frowned. 'I don't understand.'

'People will comment on us going down there together.'

'It's only a walk.' She tried to jest but it fell flat.

'They don't know that.'

'I shall tell my father.'

Harding rubbed his fingers across his forehead. 'I don't want...I don't think it's a good idea.'

She stared at him, doing her best to be reasonable. 'It's only a walk.'

'But it's with you,' he whispered.

The blood drained from her face. He'd done it again. Once more he'd slighted her. What was so wrong with *her*?

Above the steps the cellar door opened, and Owen bent to look down at them all. 'The all clear has sounded.'

General murmuring and rustling as everyone left the cellar gave Audrey the chance to recover her emotions. As she turned to go, Harding reached out, but his hand fell away before it touched her. She stared at him a moment more and then left him.

Audrey fought the disappointment stirring inside her and went outside to the barn. She needed to keep busy to stop herself from being tormented by a man she didn't understand. Never had she been so confused. She didn't know what to do or where she stood with him. One minute he was distant and the next he was trying to breach the gap. Was this some kind of game? Because if it was, she didn't know the rules.

Why did he dance with her and hold her so closely only to dismiss her when the music stopped? Why did his eyes send her messages his lips never uttered?

He attracted her, made her feel new and exciting sensations, but it come with a price - hurt and confusion. Why didn't she simply forget him, ignore him? She'd tried to, desperately wanted to, but in the end, she couldn't disregard him.

After collecting a garden fork, she headed for the kitchen vegetable garden, intent on losing herself in work for the rest of the day. If Captain Jake Harding wanted to reject her friendship, then so be it. She'd not waste another minute on struggling to comprehend it all.

'Miss Pearson!' The man she was trying to put out of her mind made his way to her from the back of the house.

She sighed, not ready for another attack of nervous tension. 'Yes?'

The Captain stopped a few feet from her, his blue eyes crinkled at the corners as he squinted into the sun. 'Would…*is* it possible for us to take that walk?'

Oh, this man was frustrating!

'I don't know, Captain. Is it?' She raised her chin, her tone sarcastic. 'After all, there *may* be gossip, and it is *me* you'll be walking with.'

He had the grace to look ashamed and stuck his hands in his trouser pockets, head bowed. 'I apologise for my lack of manners. I am not normally so…so…'

'Insensitive? Ill-mannered?'

A wry smile lifted the corners of his mouth, and Audrey's toes curled with the want to kiss him there.

'Very well, Captain. I shall take you.' She leaned the fork against the small wall surrounding the herb garden and noticed Owen in the greenhouse behind the lines of laundry. She hurried over to tell him of their walk-in case anyone came looking for them and then returned to stand beside the Captain. 'Ready?'

He nodded and they fell into step. In silence they skirted the long rows of vegetables and entered the blossoming orchard, the scent of the apple bloom heady on the still air. At the end of the orchard, Audrey opened a small gate, and they were now in the open fields, which stretched to the cliff's edge.

'It's not that far at all,' Harding murmured.

'No, it's not.' The closer to the cliffs they came the sharper the tang of salt air tasted on their lips. 'In summer, as children, we would go to the beach nearly every day. I adore it.'

At the top of the cliff, they stood and gazed out. A vista of sparkling water, shimmering sand and rocky bluffs greeted them.

'It would be nice to grow up here. You were very lucky to have such a place to roam.' Harding seemed to retreat into himself again, as though memories haunted his every waking moment.

Audrey turned from the view and studied him. The weight had dropped from him since his arrival over two weeks ago. His cheeks were hollowed, shadows bruised under his beautiful eyes. Did he sleep at all? She knew he rarely ate.

He caught her looking at him and she spun away, heading for the path leading down to the shore below. 'It looks steep, but it is quite easy. Over the years we've put in proper steps here and there and the odd handrail.'

They went down single file, slipping and sliding a little in places, where lack of use had caused the build-up of loose pebbles and sandy drifts. At the bottom, Audrey took off her shoes and socks and rolled up the legs of her overalls.

Harding watched her, smiling. 'I'll keep mine on, I think.'

'How will you paddle then?' she teased, straightening.

'I don't intend to paddle.'

She tutted, grinning. 'Imagine coming down to the beach and not getting your feet wet.'

'You have to get past all that barbed wire first.'

She headed off towards the gentle lapping waves, the sand gritty between her toes. 'We made a small entrance between two joins. Only we know where it is. No Germans would be able to see where it is.'

He strode beside her. 'Who is, we?'

Audrey stopped at the edge of the water, her feet sinking into the cold, wet sand. In front of them the ugly rolls of wire stretched along the beach. Over the last year or so, the thrashing waves had shifted the position of some of the wire, causing it to twist and bend out of shape.

'You don't have to tell me.'

'It was my brother, Robbie, Lucy and I.' She stared out over the shimmering water, dazzling in the sunlight like a thousand diamonds. 'Before Robbie joined up, the army came and put the barbed wire all along this coast. Stopping us from swimming and fishing. So, we cut it a bit for access.' She remembered that day so clearly. It was the last day of innocence for them, the last day they heard Robbie laugh.

'I know your brother was killed in battle. Your father told me.'

She jerked. 'Father has spoken to you about it?'

'Only once, but I'm hoping it'll be more. I feel he needs to talk about his loss.'

'Father won't mention Robbie's name to us. I think he tries to believe it's not true, not his boy.'

Harding nodded. 'That's a common grieving process.'

Audrey sighed, not wanting to think of sad things. 'I'm glad Father has spoken to you.' She walked away and he followed her. They hugged the water's edge, Audrey allowing the waves to wet up to her knees and the end of the overalls. Above them, a lone seagull shrieked.

'What a gorgeous day.'

'Yes…' he whispered, though he was looking at her as he spoke.

Audrey felt the connection between them again but was loath to do or say anything that would make him turn from her or possibly reject her once more. 'The beach is so soothing, isn't it?'

'I believe so. I should bring the men down here, or at least those who could manage the climb down.'

'We could have a picnic.'

He smiled, revealing even white teeth. 'Splendid idea.' He winked and her heart swelled.

They walked on, happy to be silent, enjoying their companionship. Audrey would glance at him when he looked the other way. It didn't seem real, to be walking the beach with this intelligent, handsome man, but she stopped herself from thinking more. He'd offered an olive branch; she mustn't get ahead of herself and think of it as more than it was.

'May I ask where you are from, Captain?'

'Shrewsbury.'

'What made you become a doctor?' She so much wanted to know more about him but was hesitant to ask anything too personal.

'To please my mother.' He gazed into the distance. 'No, that's not completely true. I wanted to help people, not simply make them well and forget them, but to make a difference to their lives, give them hope that there was someone who would listen to them. I wanted to give people the kind of treatment my father never got.'

'Your father?'

'Yes. You see my father died after suffering with poor health for many years and we never really understood why he couldn't be helped or cured. My father's doctor was an unkind man, didn't have an ounce of sympathy for his patients, and I grew to hate him. I thought that a doctor should never act as that man did. Thankfully, we had the funds for me to go to university. Though we aren't an overly wealthy family.'

'Your mother must be very proud.'

'Yes, she is, and I can take care of her in her old age, once this war is over.'

Suddenly, he stopped as if he'd realised he'd spoken too much of his private life. 'I should be getting back now.'

'Yes, of course.'

They retraced their steps without speaking again. Harding led the way up the cliff. Every now and then, he would turn to take Audrey's hand to help her up a difficult bit of the path. At the top they paused to catch their breath.

'Thank you for taking me.' Harding smiled. 'I enjoyed it.'

Self-conscious of him and the fluttering of her stomach, she nodded. 'You're welcome. Perhaps we can do it again some other time.'

'Perhaps…yes, I'd like that.'

Crossing the fields, Audrey noticed her father standing by the gate leading to the orchard, and as they approached, he waved his pipe at them.

'What are you doing here, Father?' She bent down and patted Max, who'd managed to trot along beside his master.

'Just taking a stroll with Max, my dear, and enjoying my smoke.' Her father puffed on his pipe. 'How did you find the walk, Captain?'

'Very good, sir. Your home is situated in a beautiful spot.'

'Indeed, it is.' Ernest wrapped his arm around Audrey. 'My girl here knows that beach better than anyone. Swims like a fish she does, too.'

'I was honoured to have her show me, sir.' Harding smiled at Audrey. 'Now, if you'll excuse me, I'd best see to my patients.'

Watching him go, Audrey felt a sense of loss. It had been wonderful to have him to herself, to have the chance to learn a little more about him.

'He's a good man,' her father murmured, sucking his pipe stem.

'Yes, he is,' she whispered. He totally fascinated her, and she knew she never wanted him out of her sight.

'He was telling me about his wife.'

Wife? Captain Harding had a wife? Audrey swayed, her stomach twisting into knots. She didn't care to know about his wife. Anger and pain mixed together; she couldn't breathe. Flustered, she tried to think of something to say to stop her father from mentioning Mrs Harding. 'Have-have you heard from Mr Samuels, Father? I hear he's bought a-a boat.'

'A boat? Why, the man doesn't know the bow from the stern!' As her father remonstrated about silly old men buying boats when they didn't know anything about them, she was able to gather her shattered thoughts and steady her erratic heartbeat. So, he had a wife. Well, now she knew, and she should be grateful that the knowledge would save her from embarrassing herself towards him. But oh, how it hurt…

Chapter Five

Jake put down his pen and gazed out the window. Rain lashed the countryside, the heavy clouds low. He hated rain, but at least the wet misty weather would keep the German planes away. Fog had shrouded the coastline for the last day, making it impossible for them to identify targets.

Two nurses passed by the door, chatting happily. He heard Sister Lewis speak to them and then their footsteps faded, and silence resumed.

Rubbing the back of his neck, Jake stretched, alert for any indication of Audrey's presence. What was he to do? He hadn't been expecting to find a woman as interesting and lovely as her, not here, not at this time in his life. The last thing he wanted was a romantic entanglement. Love had nearly killed him last time around, he couldn't stand another beating from it.

He pushed up the sleeve cuff on his left arm to expose the long red scar running from his elbow down to his wrist. It had healed well and didn't hinder his work as a doctor, thankfully, but then, physical scars healed, it was the mental ones that didn't always.

Footsteps rang through the hall. Jake paused, waiting to see if it was Audrey, though she kept outside most of the time, working until sundown. He frowned at that. Since their walk along the beach last week, he'd barely seen her, not even managed to say good day to her. Was she avoiding him? Could he blame her? He'd done his best to make her dislike him. He'd recognised the attraction between them, and it had scared him, horrified him, and he'd done his best to keep his distance, but then, even with that he had failed. She'd captured his interest and despite his wish to keep away from her, she'd unknowingly drawn him to her.

The footsteps passed, one of the officers, Winthrop probably. He often walked the halls when it was raining, like a caged lion he was, not fond of being cooped up. Well, he'd not be for much longer. Four of the officers were leaving in the morning, going back to the front.

Jake shivered at the thought and left his chair to stand by the window, hating his weakness whenever he thought of *the front*… Of what he had done…

Raindrops raced each other down the pane. Was Audrey out in this weather? Was she cold? Why did she work so hard? Laying his head against the cold glass, he sighed. He didn't want to feel attracted to her, nor did he want to think about her every waking moment.

It'd taken two years to recover from Marianne's death. Two years of hell, throwing himself with abandon into every battle he could, hoping he'd be knocked, not just wounded, but killed. Dead. Dead like Marianne and their baby that hadn't even drawn breath.

'Doctor?'

He swung around, blinking at Sister Lewis. 'I do apologise, Sister. I-I was miles away.'

She smiled; her movements efficient. She was a good nurse, competent, knowledgeable. He liked her. 'Did you need me, Sister?'

'Yes, I thought we might have a little speech at supper tonight, to wish the men that are going good luck.'

'Excellent idea.'

'Also, I need you to sign a few papers when you're ready and would you check Major Johnson, I think he's running a temperature.'

'Yes, I'll do it now.' He left the room with her and they went upstairs to the first bedroom where Major Johnson laid on his bed shivering. After his examination, Jake drew Sister Lewis to one side. 'It's likely just a bad chest cold, but I want him isolated. We can't have the whole house coming down with it, nor can we subject the men who are leaving tomorrow to it.'

'Of course.'

'Leave him in here and keep up the fluids. Move Colonel Barnes and Captain Watts to another room.'

'Very good, Doctor.'

Jake left the room, did a check of the bedrooms, but found most of them empty and the men downstairs in the dining room, where a fire had been lit and a game of cards being played. They all looked well enough, but he knew how quickly a simple chest cold could spread.

Returning to the office, he paused on hearing laughter. Lucy's high laugh made him smile. She was so different to Audrey. So full of life whereas Audrey carried the responsibilities the changes the war had brought.

'Doctor. Doctor. Captain Harding!'

The urgency of the calling had Jake spinning around. He ran to the door, colliding with Nurse Proctor in the hall. 'What's happened?'

Some of the officers had come out of rooms to see what was the emergency.

'You must come quick. It's Mr Pearson, he's sick, fallen.' She hurriedly led him upstairs into Ernest's bedroom. The old man lay sprawled on the rug beside the bed. His staring eyes told the outcome. Jake's training made him spring into action as he checked the man's pulse, but all the while he was thinking that now Audrey had lost her father too.

Sister Lewis entered and put a hand to her throat. 'Oh no. Not dear Mr Pearson. Oh, heavens no…'

Kneeling by the dead man, Jake nodded and closed the man's eyes. 'Help me lift him onto the bed.' Both Proctor and Sister Lewis helped him, and they arranged Ernest so that he looked restful. Jake glanced at Valerie. 'He's had a heart attack I would think.'

'Yes. I was expecting it. The poor man told me of his chest pains last month.'

'Will you make the arrangements? I'll get the paperwork ready.'

'Yes.' She nodded just as Lucy's laugh tinkled throughout the house. 'Poor Audrey and Lucy. It's just the two of them now.'

'They need to be told.'

'Audrey's out in the barn I think.'

'I'll go find Miss Pearson. Will you inform Miss Lucy?'

'Yes, I don't want her to come up here and find him.' They went downstairs together, parting in the hall. Jake continued on to the back corridor and in the cloakroom donned his coat. Rain lashed him the moment he stepped outside, and he ran across the yard to the barn only to have Alf tell him that Audrey was in one of the greenhouses potting plants.

By the time he had located Audrey in the furthest greenhouse, he was wet and cold. Opening the door, the humid warmth hit him like an opened oven. Silently he made his way down the length of the greenhouse. Either side of the aisle held long wooden benches full of pots, some empty, some with dirt in and some sprouting small plants.

Ten feet from the end, the benches stopped, and the area was open. Here Audrey knelt, searching through dirt, spread out on the stone floor.'

'What are you doing?' Jake murmured.

She jumped and looked up. 'You frightened me.'

'Sorry. I didn't mean to.' He indicated to the dirt. 'Have you lost something?'

She smiled. 'No. I was searching for seeds. This pot hadn't been labelled and I didn't know if it held seeds or needed to be planted.'

He hunched down beside her, dreading the news he'd have to impart. 'Can I speak with you for a moment?'

Audrey looked surprised at the request. Her soft brown eyes widened. 'Absolutely.' She took off her gardening gloves and pushed her curls from her face with the back of her hand.

Against the wall was a paint-flecked table that looked a hundred years old and an old rickety bench seat. 'Shall we sit here?' He helped her up but kept her small hand in his after she'd sat on the seat.

'Is something wrong, Captain?'

He nodded and sat beside her, wishing he could say the words without having to break her heart. 'I have bad news.'

'Is it my father?' Her gaze locked with his and he squeezed her hand.

'Yes. I'm sorry. I believe he suffered a fatal heart attack.'

She bowed her head and Jake desperately wanted to kiss the top of it and tell her it would all be all right, that he would make it better. He was astonished to feel so deeply about this kind, generous woman next to him. Caressing her hand, he studied her fingers, the nails short, blisters on her palm. Working hands. Yet, he'd seen her gently touch a solider in comfort, hold her father's hand and cradle Lucy's cheek. She was a giving woman, and he was so grateful to have been sent to her home, to have met her, know her.

'I was expecting it, have been for some time,' she whispered, not lifting her head.

He was conscious of the rain splattering against the greenhouse, but inside it they were cocooned, warm, but not without pain.

'I have to tell Lucy.' She went to rise, but he held her back.

'Sister Lewis has gone to her while I came to you.'

She stared at him, seemingly to look right through him. 'Valerie will help her accept it. She might have gone mad if I'd told her. They were so close, you see. Lucy adored Father and he her. Since the war, no, before that, since Mother's death, they have been inseparable.'

Jake knew she didn't need him to speak and so he held her hand in both of his, hoping to give her some of his strength to make it through this ordeal. Death was so final. There were no second chances.

He watched, fascinated, as a solitary tear slipped over her lashes and trickled down her cheek. Automatically he caught it with his fingertip.

'We are alone now, Lucy and I.' Audrey looked away. 'Just the two of us. Sometimes it seems like only yesterday we were all together, laughing around the piano at Christmas. Robbie played the piano wonderfully well and we'd dance for hours…'

'It sounds like a perfect time.'

'It was.' Her chin trembled and Jake couldn't help himself, he had to comfort her. Gathering her into his arms, he held her unresisting body tight. She was so thin, dreadfully thin. Running one hand over her hair, he murmured soothing words and she sagged against him, but didn't cry.

Suddenly she sprang away, rose and walked over to the benches. 'I-I must go to Lucy.'

He stood, watching her pale face and the naked emotions flickering across it. 'If you ever want to talk, please come to me. I will help all I can.'

'You're very kind, but I will be quite all right.' She shrugged one shoulder as though it meant nothing. 'Thank you for your concern.'

He ached to hold her again, but he had no right. 'You don't have to do this alone.'

'I'm not alone. I have Lucy and Valerie.' She walked away.

Jake took a step, silently shouting she had him too, but his emotions had been frozen for too long. He couldn't do anything rash, couldn't think too far ahead. She needed a man to love her properly. What did he have to offer? A broken shell of what he once was?

Stiffly he sat back down. She didn't need him. He knew enough about men's mental state to know he wasn't ready to take on another person's suffering too. Not so long ago, he'd been a man who cared so little for his own life he'd volunteered for every dangerous mission possible. How could he comfort her when nightmares still haunted him?

Chapter Six

Such heat. Audrey pulled her black skirt away from her legs, trying to get a little cooler. The wake had ended an hour ago and many of the guests, elderly friends of the family had all gone home. The officers had disappeared to their own rooms or out into the garden to sit under the trees in the shade. The funeral had gone well, the gathering large and the service full of warmth. Despite her own sadness and comforting Lucy, she was aware of Captain Harding's quiet support. She often caught his tender gaze, and, although it was kind of him, it didn't really help her. Inside, she felt hollow. Was it so wrong of her to want the strong arms of a man's comfort — a man she couldn't have? Why couldn't she put him from her head and heart?

Collecting the last plates and glasses, Audrey left the dining room and went to the kitchen. There, Lucy helped Mrs Graham wash up, while young Betsy chopped vegetables for the evening stew.

'Is that the last of it, pet?' Mrs Graham took the tray from her and bustled back to the sink.

'Yes, it is. I'll sweep the dining room floor now.'

'No, you won't. I'll get Betsy to do that when she's finished with the vegetables. You go up and lie down for a while. You've been up since dawn.'

The thought of lying down in a hot airless room didn't appeal. 'I think I might go for a walk along the beach. Want to come Lucy?'

Lucy turned from the cupboard where she was stacking plates and shook her head. 'I might lie down. I haven't been sleeping well.'

Mrs Graham placed her hand on Lucy's arm. 'Leave that, my dear, and go on up. If you miss your tea, I'll keep a tray for you for later.'

'Thank you, Mrs Graham.' Lucy kissed her cheek and then came to kiss Audrey. 'Enjoy your walk.'

Audrey stepped outside and turned her face up to the sun. She enjoyed June weather, usually hot days with perhaps a thunderstorm in the evening. Summer meant lazy hours at the beach or bicycling through the countryside, having picnics, but that seemed so long ago.

'What are you doing standing there?' Valerie smiled at her.

'I'm off for a walk. Want to come?'

Shaking her head, Valerie took a step inside. 'It's too hot. Besides, I'm on duty in about ten minutes.'

'I feel I've hardly spoken to you in the last few days.'

Valerie embraced her. 'I'm sorry. We'll have to fix that. How about we go to the movies tomorrow?'

Audrey smiled. 'Lovely.'

'Well, I best go in. Captain Harding has been unbearable for the last day or so.'

'Oh?' Her heart beat uncomfortably. 'Why is that?'

'Who knows, but he's driving me crazy.' Grinning, Valerie leaned closer. 'If he'd only smile a bit more, I might be tempted to fall in love with him.'

Audrey froze, shattered by her dearest friend's words.

'I was joking.' Valerie chuckled as though it was a huge joke, but then the smile slipped from her face. 'Oh, Audrey, I didn't mean it, honestly. I want no man, not now or ever.' Then her eyes widened. 'Lord, no. Oh, Audrey tell me what I'm thinking isn't true. You aren't in love with Captain Harding?'

Blinking, Audrey stepped away, forcing herself to look bemused. 'What? Oh no. No. Don't be silly.'

Val's eyes softened. 'You love him, don't you?'

'You're being ridiculous. Of course not.'

'I can see it on your face.'

Tears welled and Audrey groaned inwardly. 'Nonsense.'

'Don't lie. Not to me.'

Audrey twisted her hands together, ashamed, embarrassed and terribly confused. 'I don't know what I feel. He's so…'

'Complex?' Valerie gave her an understanding smile.

'Married.'

'He is?' Frowning, Valerie nibbled her fingernail. 'I didn't realise. Are you sure? He never mentions his family. But then, he rarely talks of anything private.'

'He spoke of his wife to Father.'

'Amazing.'

Her heart felt as heavy as lead. 'I'm going for my walk.'

'Aud-'

Audrey kissed her cheek. 'I'm fine, really. Totally perfect. Now go and we'll have a cup of tea together later.' She turned away and strode across the gardens, heading for the cliffs. The more distance she put between herself and the house the better. For days she'd been cooped up inside, handling the funeral arrangements, accepting the sympathy from all within the house and supporting Lucy. She needed time alone. Time to think.

At the top of the cliff, she paused and stared out. The sea was a beautiful blue-green, the sky cloudless. The image of Jake's smiling face shimmered on the horizon, swelling her heart with emotion and want. She yearned for the man. It was like a sickness. Recalling the day he held her, comforted her when she needed it, she closed her eyes and remembered how good it felt to be in his arms. The solidness of his chest, the sandalwood scent of him.

Sucking in a deep breath, she spread her arms out wide. What did it matter that she loved Jake Harding, a married man? Tomorrow, or even tonight, a bomb could land on them and that would be it. Gone. In a blink of an eye everything turned to dust.

Abruptly, full of energy, she scrambled down the cliff path, going faster than she'd ever done before. Slipping and sliding, she made it to the bottom with only a few scratches on her palms. After kicking off her shoes and peeling off her stockings, she ran along the beach, the sand hot beneath her toes. The cool water licked at her feet and she stomped about, wetting her skirt, before running off in the other direction.

When finally exhausted, she flopped down onto the warm sand and lay panting. It'd felt so good. Maybe that's what she had to do once in a while, simply run and twirl and splash about, behave like a child again.

A shadow fell across her face. She squinted up, jerking in alarm at the figure she couldn't make out because the sun behind him blinded her.

'Sorry to intrude.' Captain Harding knelt.

Sitting up, Audrey straightened her skirt, brushing sand off. 'I didn't see you…'

'All that larking about, I suppose.' His wry smiled made her blush. 'Can I sit with you for a while?'

'Yes.'

They sat staring out at the sea for several minutes. Audrey enjoyed the quiet peacefulness. Again, she felt comfortable with him, the sense of not having to make conversation. Was she doing this wrong? Should she flirt and giggle like other girls did? Would that make him notice her as a woman? But then he had a wife…

Jake shifted on the sand, his arms resting lightly on top of his bent knees. 'I admire you.'

'Really?' She glanced at him in surprise, before ducking her head to play with the sand. 'I've done nothing exceptional, nothing admirable.'

'You've kept strong in difficult circumstances. It's hard enough losing a parent without also having a house full of strangers to contend with.'

'I have no choice about that. There's no point whining over something I can't change. Besides, I must be strong, for Lucy's sake.'

'Lucy is stronger than you think.'

She nodded. 'Yes, I know, but looking after her is a habit of mine. Though the day will come when she won't need me.'

Silence stretched again. Seagulls soared on the air currents.

'Why did you apply to have soldiers here?' he asked.

'My Grandfather was in the Navy, and Father served in the Boer and Great War. He felt it was the least he could do for this war, as he was too old to do anything else. The thought of giving men a welcoming place to heal gave him great satisfaction.'

'Is that why you have a house near the water, having sailors in the family?'

Audrey smiled. 'Yes. Grandfather built Twelve Pines when he was a young man. His father made a tremendous amount of money in shipping and property. Apparently, Grandfather joined the navy to escape sitting in an office and running the business. He saw this part of the coast from out there.' She pointed out to sea. 'When he docked in Hull, he came here and bought the land immediately from a farmer.'

'It's a beautiful spot.'

'Agreed.'

'And now it's yours and Lucy's.'

'Yes.' She let the sand drift through her fingers. 'Though I'd give it all away if it meant I could have my family back.'

'It's no good to dwell on the past. Think to the future.'

'Is that your professional opinion?' She looked at him.

'Yes, it can be.' He frowned. 'It can also be from someone who knows.'

'What future? I feel I don't have much of a future. Lucy will one day marry and likely leave the area. She's wanted to travel for so long.' Audrey frowned at the thought of Lucy leaving one day. 'I could end up an old maid alone in a huge house. That's no fun.'

'You'll marry. Someone like you doesn't stay single forever.'

Her eyes widened. What did he mean? 'Someone like me?'

'That wasn't an insult. I meant someone clever and lovely as you.'

'I won't marry.' She was certain of that. How could any man compare to the dashing captain sitting beside her? He thought her clever and lovely. She tingled inside. One look from him sent her to another world. There couldn't be two men on this earth who could have that ability, surely. She gazed at him. 'I doubt there will be many men left to marry after this war anyway.'

He took her hand, gritty with sand. 'Someone will steal your heart.'

Her heart had already been stolen, not that it would do her any good. Audrey slipped her hand out from his. His touch gave her butterflies in her stomach, made it hard to think rationally. She had to steer the conversation to safer topics. 'Do you receive letters from your mother?'

Jake turned to face the water again. 'Occasionally, yes.'

'You could invite her here, if you like? We have room until new soldiers arrive.'

'I don't think so. She's better being where she is. Her cousin lives across the street from her and they spend much of their time together. Keep each other company.'

'What about your wife?' Audrey swallowed. 'She-she could come.'

Slowly, as though movement caused him pain, Jake turned to stare at her. 'Who told you I was married?'

'My father.'

His fierce expression frightened her. 'I see.'

'Did he break a confidence? I'm sorry if he-'

'No!' He stood, dusting the sand from his trousers in short jerky movements.

'Captain, I-'

'I have to return to the house.'

'Forgive me. I didn't mean to pry or upset you.'

He took a step and faltered, his hands clenching at his sides. 'My wife…my wife is dead.'

'Oh. I'm so sorry.' She rose, feeling sad for the pain that shadowed his beautiful blue eyes. 'I didn't know.'

'Why should you? It's my private business. It doesn't concern anyone but me.'

'Of course.' She glanced away, unable to bear his cold expression.

'I'm sorry.' Jake ran his fingers through his short dark hair. 'It's not something I feel comfortable talking about.'

'It's understandable. I apologise for bringing it up.'

'My wife meant everything to me. She was the reason for my being…the reason I lived.'

Audrey's heart was breaking as the stark emotion criss-crossed his handsome face. He was still in mourning…still in love with his wife. How could she even try to compete with a dead woman? 'She sounds like a wonderful person.'

His stiff shoulders relaxed. 'She was. Marianne…that was her name.'

'A beautiful name.' She smiled, loving him and knowing she was free to love him, even if *his* heart was closed to that emotion at the moment.

'You would have liked her, Audrey, may I call you Audrey?'

'I would like that, yes.'

He held out his hand and warmth returned to his eyes. 'I'm Jake.'

She placed her hand in his. 'Jake. Shall we sit down again?'

They settled back in the sand and Audrey ignored the damage the fine grit would do to her skirt. Instead, she concentrated on the intriguing man next to her. 'Can you speak about Marianne? I'd like to know about her, but you don't have to, of course. If it's too painful.'

Jake looked out over the water. 'There's a boat out there.'

Audrey followed his gaze, spotting a boat on the horizon, probably a fishing trawler or mine sweeper.

'She died trying to bring our baby into the world.'

Audrey remained silent, watching the boat. Instinct told her Jake needed to talk and for someone to listen. Perhaps her father might have played that role if he'd lived, but today it was her, and she was so glad and terribly grateful for it.

'The child was stillborn, you see. She hadn't felt the baby move for days and the doctor said it had died. Marianne was too weak with grief to survive the childbirth. She had stopped eating. She bled…they couldn't stop it…' He shrugged, as though throwing off the image. 'She'd never been strong really, always had health problems…'

'How terribly tragic.'

'I was home on leave at the time. We were so excited waiting for the baby to arrive. We were going to be a family. But then in one dreadful day I lost them both. I forgot about the war, being a doctor and everything else except losing Marianne and the baby. Instead of being a husband and father I became nothing to no one.' His voice was calm, but the muscle ticking along his jaw revealed his inner torment.

'When did this happen?'

'Four years ago. January 5th, nineteen forty. Sometimes it feels like yesterday, and at other times, it is as though it never happened, but in a dream.' He swallowed and took a deep breath. 'So, now you know.'

'It helps me to know, Jake. Makes me understand you better.'

'My moods, you mean.' His wry grin appeared. 'I know I can be insufferable. I'm sorry for that.'

'We can all be unbearable at times. Do you feel better for telling me or worse?'

'I'm not certain.'

'Shall we go for a walk?' She rose and shook off the sand.

Jake stood also and faced her. 'I should be going back. Doctor Penshaw has invited me to a meal at his home. No doubt he's wishing to talk about all things medical.' Gently he cupped her cheek, his thumb caressing her skin. 'You are a special person, Audrey Pearson. On this day when you've buried your father, you've listened to another's sorrow.'

She gazed into his eyes, which had softened and become the shade of lavender. Her breathing slowed and time was suspended between them. 'I don't want you to suffer your sorrow alone anymore, Jake. I want to be a comfort to you.'

He smiled, but it didn't reach his eyes and he dropped his hand. 'One can never have enough friends.'

Her heart twisted at his words. Friends. He wanted friendship. She wanted so much more. Would he ever think of love again? Could she show him her devotion — she who had never been in love before?

Chapter Seven

Audrey turned the knob on the wireless. Behind her the drawing room was full, every member of the household waited to hear the news. Static noise filled the room, some of the soldiers winced. After a few adjustments, the sonorous voice became clear. In silence, they listened to the announcement of the D-Day landings in Normandy. It was hard to comprehend the vastness of such an invasion. Her gaze roamed the men's faces. Each one of them wore a haunted expression and her heart turned over in sympathy for them.

'That'll sort out those German blighters!' Colonel Barnes declared when the announcement was over, and music replaced the voice. 'Churchill will see us through, never fear.'

'Well, something has to happen to finish it.' Major Johnson murmured, standing up from the armchair. His chest cold had left him weak and thin. He left the room with some of the officers.

Audrey watched them go, knowing their mixed emotions. Some hated being left out of such a battle while others were glad to be safe here. Jake stood by the door and their eyes met as the staff left to return to their duties. He gave her a small smile, lingering a moment more before walking away. What was he thinking?

'Just think of all those casualties,' Nurse Williams whispered, wiping away a tear as she and the other nurses left.

'Audrey, can we go to the cinema now? I'm so bored.' Lucy sat on the window seat, filing her nails. 'We can catch the late screening.'

'Heavens Lucy, show some compassion. You talk of films while thousands of men are fighting in battle, lying dead on foreign beaches.'

Lucy blushed. 'I *am* sensitive to their plight, but there's nothing I can do about it. We must go on living in this horrid war. Why should I be miserable? Would the soldiers want me to be?' She tossed back her curls. 'I think the servicemen would be happy to know their girls are enjoying something. Doesn't the army say we have to keep up morale, be happy for when the men return?'

Audrey shook her head. Her sister knew how to debate any argument. 'Do we have to go tonight?'

'Yes. I want some cheering up and to forget this Normandy battle and all the men who've died. It's all too wretched.'

'I really don't feel like it.' Turning the wireless off, Audrey yawned. She wasn't sleeping well, her nights broken with images of Jake. Often dawn arrived with her sitting by the bedroom window wrapped in a blanket, thinking about a man who slept under the same roof, but who might as well have been

82

miles away, such was the distance he put between them. She wondered if she could climb those emotional walls he built.

'What are you two up to?' Valerie came into the room from the office across the hall.

'Audrey won't come with me to the cinema.' Lucy pouted like a child. 'I so want to see the new Bing Crosby film, *Going My Way*.'

'Bing Crosby?' Valerie's eyes widened. 'May I come too? I'm off duty. His voice is beautiful.'

Audrey grinned at them both. 'You two go. I'll stay home.'

'You don't want to stay home, Audrey. You need some relief from all this too.' Valerie sat on the arm of one of the armchairs. 'Why don't the three of us make a night of it? Have tea out somewhere in Bridlington then go to the pictures.'

'Oh, splendid idea, Val.' Lucy slipped the nail file into her pocket. 'I'll tell Owen to bring the car around and then I'll get changed.'

'Do we have enough petrol rations?'

Lucy kissed Audrey's cheek. 'Owen always has enough of everything. He just wants us to think he doesn't.'

'I'm not going, Lucy.' Audrey forestalled her. 'Go with Val, but I'm not going. I think I'll have a long hot bath instead. I have some of father's accounts I need to look over. So, I might take them to bed with me and have an early night.'

Val patted Audrey's hand. 'That might suit you best.'

After helping Lucy change and then waving both of them off, Audrey lay soaking in a hot tub. She broke the war rules, which stated she had to use only four inches of water, but for once she didn't care about rules and regulations. Valerie had given her some bath crystals and their perfume scented the air and Audrey's skin. She'd washed her hair, soaped her body and now reclined, relaxing.

Outside night had fallen, and blackout made every room even darker. Audrey had broken her own rules of being stringent with supplies and extravagantly lit six candles, placing them around the bath. The golden flickering glow gave her skin a healthy sheen, the water shimmered in the semi-light.

Gazing down at her body, Audrey tried to scrutinise it from a man's point of view. She had slender legs, her hips weren't too wide, but hopefully wide enough should she ever have to give birth. Running her hands down her chest she cupped her breasts. Were they too small? She'd never thought them huge, nor were they tiny. What did men prefer? It was something she'd never considered before. Her breasts were simply there and never much thought of. She studied the soft pink nipples. They weren't very attractive. Did it matter?

Gripping her waist, she tried to get her hands to meet. When she'd last been fitted for a dress, before the war, her waist had measured twenty-five inches. But she knew she'd lost weight, her skirt bands gaped. She'd easily be a twenty-two inch waist now. Was she too thin? Did men like their women with more weight, large breasts, longer legs?

What did Jake like? Had his wife been a beauty with a perfect figure?

Audrey's head swam with uncertainty. She slipped further down into the water and closed her eyes. What did it matter anyway? If Jake didn't want more than friendship, her body was never going to be an issue.

Still, it would be nice to be held by him, touched by him. His hands caressing her breasts…

The image had her shooting upright, blushing. She throbbed between her legs. Lord, she was a fool. Such improper thoughts. Lusting after a man. Where would that get her? She'd gone to school with a girl who was boy mad, couldn't get enough of them. And look what happened to her? She ended up pregnant at seventeen and abandoned, her parents sending her away to some aunt in Scotland.

Audrey let out a breath. She wasn't seventeen, but twenty-four. A woman with means, an eligible woman, some would say a catch for any man. Only, she wanted just one particular man. Jake Harding. She was *in love* with Jake.

Getting out of the bath, she grabbed the towel and dried herself. Annoyed and a little teary, she blew out five of the candles, giving her enough light to get dress by. Her long nightgown flowed down to her toes, soft from constant washing and wearing. She slipped on her dressing gown and tied the belt.

Suddenly the thin wail of the air raid siren broke the quiet. Audrey groaned. Blasted bombings! Another night disrupted and hours spent in the cellar. She heard running footsteps outside the door. The whistle of a bomb split the air. The house shook as it landed nearby. The shock of a bomb so close kept her immobile for a moment. A shout in the hallway sprang her into action.

Flinging open the door, Audrey prayed Lucy and Val would be safe and then raced downstairs, only to realise she was in her night wear. She couldn't spend the night in the cellar in her nightgown, not with Jake in the same room. She turned and raced back up the stairs to her room. She stripped off the nightgown, her fingers tangling her underwear as she hopped about the room putting it on. The buttons on her white blouse refused to do up and Audrey swore just as her bedroom door opened.

'Audrey?'

'I'm coming. Won't be-' She turned to stare at Jake. His eyes widened at her bare legs, silky French knickers.

A muscle ticked along his jaw; he didn't move. His eyes lingered on her body.

Desire flooded her, making her shake. She ached for him to hold her, desperate for his lips on hers. She forgot about everything but his presence in her room. He took a hesitant step towards her and it was enough to send her running into his arms.

She kissed him hard, wanting to stamp her owner-ship on him. Jake's arms encircled her tight, like a band of steel nearly cracking her ribs, but she didn't care and glorified in the abandonment of his normal control. The kiss was long, searching, bonding them together as naturally as the sun rising.

Arching into him, she gasped as he broke off the kiss to nibble her ear and then kiss her neck. His strong hands ran down her body, moulding her shape to his. She shivered as his hands cupped her silk clad bottom, pressing her into him. She felt him hard against her and her inner core throbbed. Threading her fingers through his hair, she brought his mouth back to hers. She couldn't get enough of him. Some-thing hot and pounding between her legs took over her brain. She undid the buttons of his shirt, wanting to feel his bare skin against hers.

Another blast made the house shudder. There was a sound of breaking glass, a man yelling.

Jake tore his mouth from hers, breathing heavily. 'Audrey.'

'Don't stop...' She pulled his shirt out from his trousers, lost in a fog of need. She brought his mouth back to hers, cupping his face, keeping him with her. It'd seemed like she'd waited her whole life for this, for him.

'No, Audrey.' Jake stepped back, dropping his hands as a man's scream came again.

Blinking, trying to focus, Audrey watched as Jake tucked his shirt back in, edging his way to the door. 'I have to go. Nielson-'

'But Jake...'

His face looked pained. 'I can't...' The man's yelling came again. 'That's Nielson. I have to go. Get down to the cellar.' Then he was gone, and Audrey stood shivering, confused and frightened by the enormity of her feelings.

The drone of planes above broke her out of her dream-like state, and she pulled on black slacks with shaking fingers.

What had she done?

She groaned, and despite the danger outside she sat on the bed, utterly drained and shattered. Her hands shook and she clasped them together in her lap. The hollowness she felt was nothing like she'd ever experienced before. For the first time in her life, she felt completely alone.

Nielson's screams shot her upright. As much as she longed to crawl into bed and sob her heart out, she couldn't. She had to get down to the cellar and help the others. Tucking in her blouse, she ran downstairs only to collide with nurse Williams at the bottom, nearly knocking the medicine tray out of her hands. 'What are you doing? Go to the cellar!'

'I can't Miss Pearson.' Williams stepped past her. 'Lieutenant Nielson won't come out of his room. The doctor is with him, but he needs this medicine and Sister Lewis isn't here.'

Nielson's screams came again, filling the house.

'I'll go. You go help in the cellar.' Audrey took the small tray from her, turned and ran back up the stairs. She could hear the clack clack of the anti-aircraft guns in the distance. Opening the door to Sid Nielson's bedroom, she found the young man huddled in the corner, his arms over his head. Jake crouched before him talking quietly. He didn't turn to see who'd come into the room but concentrated on helping the afflicted man.

Now she was here, Audrey didn't know what to do. She placed the tray carefully on the bedside table.

'Now, Sid, just relax,' Jake murmured, his tone soft, undemanding. 'When this is over, we'll have a cup of tea, yes? Perhaps Mrs Graham has baked a cake for us to enjoy.'

Nielson rocked, humming, his eyes tightly closed.

Jake crept closer. 'In the morning we should have a stroll down by the sea. What do you think? It's very peaceful down there. Think of that water, Sid, the little waves rolling onto the sand. We might see some birds nesting on the cliffs. Shall we take the binoculars?'

Slowly, Nielson lowered his arms, though he continued to rock and hum.

'Can you tell me your thoughts, Sid?' Jake whispered.

'No...' His eyes squeezed tighter.

'That's fine. Utterly fine.'

'I won't do it, you know. I won't go back. You can't make me!'

'I won't make you do anything at all. You can trust me.'

Nielson wiped his hands on his pyjama shirt. 'I can't get the blood off. It won't come off.'

'There's no blood on your hands, Sid. You're here at Twelve Pines, remember?'

'T-Twelve Pines?' Nielson opened his eyes, blinking rapidly.

'That's right.'

'Lucy is at Twelve Pines. She laughs a lot.'

Jake nodded. 'Yes, Lucy laughs a lot. We can listen to her laugh in the morning.' He turned for the medicine on the tray and caught sight of Audrey. He stared at her, his face expressionless, and then poured the medicine into a glass of water. 'Here we are, Sid. A nice drink for you, to help you settle.' He handed him the glass and watched him drink it. 'Would a sleep be welcome now, do you think?'

'Yes. I'm tired, but I don't like to sleep.'

'Why?'

'Things happen…dreams…so real…'

Jake patted his arm. 'Dreams can't hurt you, Sid. I told you that, remember? Would you feel better if I sat with you tonight? Perhaps then you won't dream, and if you do, then I'll be here for you.'

Nielson looked over Jake's shoulder to Audrey, his eyes focusing. 'Miss-Miss Pearson.'

'Good evening, Nielson.' She gave him a warm smile and went to straighten his bed sheets, turning the blankets back for him. Outside, the all clear sounded and then everything was quiet.

'Thank you, Captain.' Nielson climbed into the bed, his face grey and lined with exhaustion.

'Think nothing of it, my friend.' Jake took Nielson's pulse and nodded in satisfaction. 'Good. Now rest. I'll go get an extra pillow and blanket and will be back shortly.'

'We're still going to look for birds in the morning?'

'Absolutely.' Jake smiled as Nielson's eyes closed and his head gently fell to one side.

'Let us hope he has a peaceful night now.' Audrey whispered, as she and Jake left the room. From downstairs they heard the commotion of the emptying cellar.

'I'd better check everyone is all right,' Jake said, but didn't move. He reached out and took one of her hands. 'We need to talk I think.'

'We do?' She tried to pretend she didn't know his meaning. From his sad expression, she knew it wouldn't be a talk she'd want to have. He was regretting his actions already. Well, she wasn't ashamed. She knew she loved him.

'Audrey, I can't be what you want.'

Her chest squeezed, but she raised her chin in challenge. 'You haven't tried, so how do you know?'

'You want a good man to love you. You deserve a man's love, the right man for you.'

'And what if you are the right man for me?'

'I'm not. You mustn't think I am.' He ran his hands through his short hair. 'You're young and beautiful, there's many a man who'd love you—'

'Don't patronise me.' She tossed her head, angered by his attempts to brush her aside again.

'I'm not, honestly. You're wonderful, and I wish I could be the man you need.'

'But you are! If you just allow yourself to be.' She reached out for him, only he backed away, shaking his head.

'I won't. Audrey. I'll never marry again. I couldn't stand it. I couldn't cope with the responsibility of loving someone again, of the possible pain…'

'But I love you.' There, she had said the words.

He looked appalled. 'You can't.'

'Don't tell me how I feel.'

'You don't know what love is!'

'I'm speaking from the heart, Jake. I'm not one of those girls who plays with men's feelings. I love you like I've never loved anyone else before.'

He backed away, shaking his head, his eyes haunted. 'No. I won't do this.'

'What we shared in my bedroom was special. It was meant. You can't deny that.'

Jake gave a mocking laugh. 'It was a kiss, Audrey. A simple kiss that men and women share in times of need. It leads to sex. You don't have to be in love to have sex.'

'No. I won't listen to you.'

'It's true. Don't make it out to be more than it was.'

'Why are you so certain that it meant nothing?'

'Because I know the difference.'

She felt sick. 'So, you wanted s-sex? Just any woman will do…'

He wiped a hand over his tormented face. 'No, I didn't mean…Damn, this isn't what I meant to say. Listen to me—'

'No, I won't listen to you, not until you really know what you're saying. Not until you know what you want.'

'I don't want love, Audrey.'

Emotion clogged her throat. 'Are-Are you saying you can never love me or any woman ever again?'

'Yes, I am.'

'Why?' she croaked. Lord, could there be a pain any worse than this?

'I don't want to love another woman again, not ever.' He closed his eyes momentarily. 'I wanted to die after Marianne, I nearly did. I can't do it again, Audrey, I can't suffer such…such anguish as that again…'

People were coming up the stairs, and their chatter filtering up, drove Jake away. With a last glance at her, his eyes sending his apology, he went to meet the others and resume his role of doctor and caretaker of their reason.

But what of your reason, Jake? Audrey inwardly cried. Who would save you from your self-imposed loneliness?

~ ~ ~

Audrey took an apple from the bowl on the kitchen table and tucked it into her overall pocket, then quickly pinched a warm lemon curd tart from the cooling racks while Mrs Graham's back was turned.

'I saw that, Miss,' Mrs Graham warned, without pausing in her work of putting another tray of tarts in the oven.

'You know I can't resist having one of your tarts.' Audrey laughed.

'Aye, and when you were little, I used to smack your hands for it.' Mrs Graham sniffed in disapproval as she closed the oven, her face red from the heat.

'I'm too big to be smack now,' Audrey teased and darted away up the step and into the corridor.

'You're never too old for a slap, my girl,' Mrs Graham called after her.

Once in the cloakroom, Audrey swapped her house shoes for garden boots. Max's bed was empty, and she frowned. The old dog was hardly off his blankets since her father's death. His bowl still held food in it, another surprise.

Leaving the house, she crossed the yard munching on the tasty tart and headed for the barns. A recent week of hot weather had caused the grass to grow long and she wanted to speak to Alf or Owen about mowing it. The barns were empty of both men. None of the farming equipment had been taken out. The tractor was still parked there, along with all the other machines. She crossed the lawn, hoping they were in the vegetable gardens. Passing the greenhouses, she noticed they too were empty. Where was everyone?

In the wood beyond the ornamental pond, she spied Alf, hunched over and swishing the under-growth with a long stick. Every so often, he'd stop, and whistle low.

'Have you lost something, Alf?' she called through cupped hands.

Despite his advancing years, he spun around quickly. 'Oh, no…'

Something about the way he was acting made her suspicious. She circled the pond and stood at the edge of the wood. 'What are you doing?'

'Er…' He scratched his bald head under his flat cap. 'Checking for moles.'

'Moles.'

'Aye.' He switched the grass again for good meas-ure.

'Why do you care if moles are in the wood?'

'They're getting into the vegetable gardens, mak-ing a right mess they are. Rotten vermin.'

She didn't believe him for a minute. 'Is Owen looking for moles too?'

'Er…' Alf glanced away. 'Er, I don't rightly know, Miss.'

'Do you know where he is?'

'Aye, I think he's on the tractor down in the bottom field.'

'The tractor is in the barn.'

His bushy grey eyebrows rose. 'It is?'

Audrey folded her arms. 'You are a terrible liar, Alf.'

'Nay, Miss—'

'What's going on?'

He looked cagey and fiddled with the stick. 'N-Nowt, Miss.'

Seeing his distress, she softened her stance. Alf and Owen had been working on the estate since before she was born, they were like members of her family and she loved them as such. 'Alf, please tell me.'

'Well, you see…' His Adam's apple bobbed.

'Yes?'

'It's Max.'

'Max?' She blinked. Max was the last thing she expected him to say. 'Has he done something bad? I thought he'd be too old to get into mischief now.'

Alf sighed, his drooping shoulders sagging even more. 'He's gone missing, Miss. We can't find him anywhere.'

'Missing?' She tucked a curl behind her ear. Max missing. 'He's done it before.'

'But not in the last year. Not since his arthritis got really bad in his back legs.'

'When was he last seen?'

'Yesterday morning. He was hobbling past the barn and I gave him a pat, as I always do.'

'Right. I'll go look for him too.' Together they walked back around the pond and into the yard. 'All of the outbuildings have been searched, I assume?'

'Aye, Miss.' Alf took another look behind bales of hay stacked to one side of the barn. 'It's not like him to not eat his dinner and we noticed he'd left all his food last night.'

Worried now, Audrey chewed a fingernail and went back out into the yard. 'He was always Father's shadow, went everywhere with him. I've neglected him since Father died. I bet he's been fretting.'

'Maybe, he has, poor old fella.'

'I should have paid more attention to him once father went.' She cursed her selfishness. All she'd been thinking about lately was the handsome Captain Harding.

'He's also old, Miss. Fifteen is a good age for a working dog.'

'I'll check the front of the house. Where's Owen searching?'

'The orchard and then sweeping out towards the cliff path.' Alf tapped his stick on the ground. 'I'll have another look around the greenhouses.'

They parted and Audrey strode around to the front of the house. Max had been her father's dog, but also loved by them all. Lucy would be upset if anything happened to him, but, after her father, Audrey was the closest to the dog, and she didn't want to think how upset she'd be too.

On the gravelled drive, she paused to scan the area. No Max. She headed off down towards the road and into the shade of the great Scots Pine trees that gave the estate its name and which also lined the drive. Halfway down the drive, she detoured across the lawns and checked the shrubbery edging one of the boundaries. Huge rhododendrons created a thick hedge and Audrey worked her way from the top down to the driveway gate, searching underneath them. At the gate she stopped and, hands on hips, gazed around.

'Audrey?' She turned and looked up the drive. Captain Harding was walking down. 'I saw you from the window. Is something wrong?'

Her toes curled as they always did on seeing him. That he'd made a special trip down the drive to inquire about what she was doing, sparked a flicker of hope. 'Yes, Max has gone missing.'

'Your father's dog?'

'Yes.' Conscious of his presence, his nearness, she struggled to think rationally, which annoyed her.

'I take it everywhere has been searched already?'

She nodded, went through the open gates and stood near the road. Turning to speak to the Captain as he joined her, she caught sight of a shape by the fence. 'Oh!'

In front of the fence, half hidden in the long grass, Max lay. Audrey slowly walked to him, knowing he was dead. Max would never willingly lay there. She knelt be his head and stroked his neck. 'There you are, old boy.'

Jake stood behind her. 'What would make him come down here?'

Audrey glanced up the road and fought tears. Without a doubt she knew what Max had been doing. 'This is the road to Bridlington. The road to the graveyard, where father is.'

'So?'

'Max was going to Father.' She believed that implicitly.

'No, he wouldn't have.' Harding didn't sound convinced. 'he might have been hit by a car.'

'I don't think so. I think he died of old age and missing Father.' She gazed up at him. 'He was my

Father's partner in every he did around the estate. Why wouldn't he want to die where he is?'

Jake reached down, took her hand and helped her to stand again. 'Are you sure? It seems a little doubtful. How would Max possibly know where you father is?'

'They sense these things, don't they? Remember Max sitting beside the driveway next to Alf when the hearse drove away with Father. Why wouldn't Max want to be with him when he knew it was his time to go?' She could tell by his expression that he didn't believe a word of it, but it didn't matter, she was content to have her hand in his warm one. It was some comfort. Sighing, she looked back up the drive. 'I'll have to go find Alf and Owen.'

'Let me.' He dropped her hand and took a step. 'You stay here with Max.'

She knelt in the grass and stroked Max's black coat. It had lost its shine of youth, but to her, he was still lovely old Max. 'I know you were trying to be with father, boy. You're a good loyal fellow and I'll miss you.' Tears smarted, and she wiped her eyes with her forearm.

A minute later, the three men returned with Owen pushing the wheelbarrow. Audrey stood to one side and watched as Max was lifted into it and then they made a slow procession back to the barn.

'There's a chaff bag folded on that shelf there, Alf, we'll put him in that.' Owen murmured, collecting a shovel from a hook. 'I'll dig a hole, Miss.'

'In the pond garden, Owen.' She followed them out. 'He loved laying by the pond and watching the carp. He never achieved his dream of catching one though.'

'Aye.' Alf nodded in agreement. 'Remember that time Mr Pearson threw him in. Max thought he'd died and gone to heaven...' His smile slipped away at the mention of heaven.

Audrey grinned. 'And Mother went crazy, saying he'd kill her precious fish. She was furious with Father.'

They went around to the pond and, in the garden that surrounded three sides of it, Owen picked a spot next to a row of lettuce seedlings. 'I was saving this spot to plant some radishes, but I hate radishes. Max is a far better choice.'

'Mother had beautiful hellebores along here,' she whispered.

'It'll be beautiful once more in time to come.' Jake smiled at her. 'One day you'll be able to replant all your mother's favourites.'

'I hope I'm alive to see it.' Alf wiped his eyes with a crumpled handkerchief.

'Did you want me to find your sister?'

She smiled her thanks to Jake but shook her head. 'She's gone into town with friends.'

In silence they watched Owen bury Max and tap the soil back into place. All over. In the space of a few minutes, all trace was gone of the family's beloved dog.

Audrey stayed by the garden as Owen and Alf declared a pint at the pub was in order. She let them go, even though there was still more work to be done that day. What did it matter if the grass was mown today or not? Did anyone care? Tears gathered again. She was tired of being brave, of struggling to keep the estate running.

'Shall we go inside for a cup of tea?' Jake steeped closer.

She rubbed one hand over her face. 'No, thank you. I think I'll go for a walk.'

'I wish I could go with you, but I have the men waiting for me. We're having a group discussion.'

'Oh?'

'I'm having the men speak of their past, to talk about happier times.'

'Happier times,' she echoed softly. A tear trickled down her cheek. 'It seems so long ago.'

'Yes…' He wiped the tear away with his thumb.

She shivered. What wouldn't she do to have his arms around her, his lips on hers. Closing her eyes, she swayed towards him.

'Audrey…'

When she opened her eyes, he was striding away to the house. Always walking away…

Chapter Eight

The summer heat baked them as they lay on blankets beneath umbrellas on the beach. Audrey, laying on a towel, lifted her head from her arms as one of the officers yelled and a ball landed with a thud next to her feet. The men were playing cricket and were as noisy as a group of children.

Valerie reached down and picked up the ball. 'Don't you hit us, Major.'

'Wouldn't dream of it, Sister Lewis.' Johnson winked as she threw it back to him.

Lying back down, Val flicked through the newspaper. 'If the men weren't wearing all that green, we could pretend there wasn't a war on.'

'And if we ignored the barbed wire, and that you are in a nurse's uniform.' Audrey murmured, closing her eyes.

'Yes.' Val laughed, folding the newspaper away. 'Still, it's nice to have a day down here for a change.'

'Father would have been in his element, he adored playing cricket and taught the three of us to play when we were quite small. Robbie was very good at it.' She squinted up at Valerie, the sunlight too bright. 'If Father was here now, he'd be telling the men how to play the game properly, how to make the correct shots.'

'Yes, he would.' Val chuckled. 'But the officers aren't doing too badly at it. They're enjoying themselves.'

'So, they should, the amount of food they've eaten today.'

'You're supposed to over-eat at picnics, silly.'

'I don't mind. Soon they'll be back in the trenches eating bully beef from a tin.'

'Majors Johnson, Pope and Evans leave on Tuesday.'

Audrey squinted at her; the sunlight harsh. 'Are we getting replacements?'

'Likely. When though, who knows.' Val poured herself a drink as the men roared, 'catch it!' and Lieutenant Price was out, caught by Lucy of all people.

Audrey smiled at them, clapping Lucy's efforts while the men took the opportunity to hug and kiss her in thanks. Even Nielson was grinning and joining in, the troubled look gone from his face for a moment. 'She's loving all that attention. Stops her from whinging she's bored and that her life isn't exciting.'

Val grinned. 'I'm surprised she hasn't fallen in love with any of the men we've had here. She's had enough to choose from.'

'I think she's too afraid to.' She sighed, swatting away a fly. 'Lucy knows, as we all do, that to love a fighting man means possibly losing him. We lost Robbie so easily. One minute he was with us, then next gone. Robbie was so handsome and full of life, when he died it brought home to us that the war isn't particular, it'll take the good and the bad. Robbie will never be with us again. We'll never laugh with him or sing at the piano with him. Lucy doesn't want to feel that loss with some young man.'

'There's many who feel the same.'

'We've lost three family members in five years. It's too callous.' She sighed. 'So, Lucy flirts and pretends to love all the men, but inside I know she's waiting for this madness to be over, and she is afraid, afraid that she'll never find someone when it is.'

Valerie studied her nails. 'There will be a special man who will come into her life when she least expects it. Lucy's sensible to wait.'

Audrey drew up her legs and hugged her knees. 'People die all the time, whether there is a war on or not. I think she should take her happiness when she can. You never know what's around the corner.' Her thoughts drifted to Jake. He too was afraid to love again.

'I agree to a point.' Sipping her drink, Valerie stared out over the sea. 'Sometimes being rash only leads to pain.'

'I think I would like to be rash, you know, every now and then. Sometimes I want to throw caution to the wind. I've always been terribly sensible and reliable.'

'There's nothing wrong being like that. I was so silly as a girl.'

'Really?' Audrey smiled. 'I can't imagine it, not you, stern Sister Lewis.'

Valerie looked at her, her manner serious. 'Tell me, have you ever fallen in love with someone so completely that you'll do anything for them?'

'Yes,' she whispered, instantly thinking of Jake and the overwhelming love she felt for him, a love she never expected to have.

'I did too. When I was seventeen.' Valerie's voice dropped and Audrey leaned closer to hear it over the noise of the cricket players. 'I was so foolish back then, and I paid for it, dearly.'

'In what way?'

Valerie shuddered and sighed deeply. 'Have you ever wondered why I am a Sister, at my age?'

Blinking at the change of conversation, she shook her head. 'Sorry, I haven't.'

'I went into nursing at eighteen.' Valerie's grey eyes darkened to the colour of storm clouds. 'I worked like someone possessed for the first four years so that I could better myself, my position and forget my past.'

'Why?'

'Because of a man, of being rash!' Valerie turned away to watch the players.

Questions tumbled into Audrey's mind, but she remained silent. Valerie's bitter statement hinted at a past Audrey had no idea about. She knew little things about Valerie, like she came from a village on the outskirts of Leeds, she was one of four children, all girls. Her father was a miner, her mother a seam-stress, but she never guessed that as a young woman Val had been hurt in love. What kind of friend was she to not know everything about her? She'd have to do better, make more of an effort to allow Val to open up and talk should she want to.

'What a wretched emotion love is.' Audrey rested her chin on her knees, knowing of her own heartache. Jake didn't want to love her or couldn't. So how was she to overcome it? Forget him or try to change his mind? 'I sometimes think we'd be better off without it at all.'

Valerie reached out her hand and gripped Audrey's. 'No, don't say that, Aud. Love can be wonderful, inspiring, and yes, it can hurt. But as the old saying goes, it's better to have loved and lost then never to have loved at all.'

'You honestly believe that?'

Valerie had no time to answer as the ball came flying over to them and landed in the middle of the blanket of food, smashing a bowl full of stewed apples, which sprayed over Valerie's skirt. She jumped up. 'Oh! Now look!'

There was a flurry of men, hot and sweaty, apologising and blaming each other with offers to help wipe up the mess, while Audrey did her best not to chuckle at the scene.

'You must all have a drink before you pass out with heat exhaustion.' She took out the cups and glasses from the basket. 'Lieutenant Price could you bring me the bottles of soft drink, please?'

He did as she asked, running down to the wet sand, where they had previously nestled the bottles to keep them cool. The talk and laughter swelled as she passed around drinks and plates of Mrs Graham's oat biscuits.

'Oh, here comes Captain Harding.' Valerie looked over to where Jake climbed down the cliff. 'He made it after all. Paperwork is such a dreary waste of time.'

Rising from the blanket, Audrey ignored the way her stomach flipped, she also ignored the figure walking towards them across the sand. Since the day they buried Max, Jake had gone out of his way to be distant and barely ever in her company. His rejection hurt and she often laid awake at night wondering if he meant it. He'd been crushed by his wife's death, and while she understood how hard it must be to stop grieving, she also knew that to wallow in it wasn't healthy either. He had honoured his wife for four years. Did he intend to mourn for the rest of his life?

Some inborn instinct told her that this man was for her—that she'd been waiting for him. She wouldn't give up. He was worth fighting for. All it took was perseverance. She wouldn't allow him to wallow in self-pity. He had to be shown that it was safe to love her, she wouldn't leave him, and if he was too stubborn to acknowledge it, then she would draw it out of him with some old-fashioned jealousy. She knew he was attracted to her, so now she had to use that to her advantage. All she had to do was play-act. Surely that wasn't too hard now, was it?

Audrey reached for her straw hat and put her plan into action. 'I think it's time I showed these men how to play cricket. Who will be my partner?'

There was a roar of approval and then the men gulped their drinks down, ready to start another game.

Colonel Barnes picked up the other bat, his skin reddening. 'I may be an old trout, but I'd be honoured to be at the other end, Miss Pearson.'

'Indeed, Colonel, I think that would be very suitable.' Since her father's funeral she had noticed a change in the old colonel and Val had told her of his long talks with Jake, which had led to the colonel wanting to re-join his regiment, if only to be used in the office or a similar position.

She picked up the cricket bat, and took her place in front of the stumps, waiting for the bowler to run in.

'You show them, Aud!' Lucy called from where she was fielding on the edge of the water.

Audrey grinned. The sun was hot, turning the sand to fire. She could feel the skin on her legs burning, but at least she tanned well. Today she wore navy shorts and a lemon short-sleeved shirt. Her curls were wild about her head and she quickly tucked them under her hat.

From the corner of her eye, she spotted Jake and Val chatting on the blanket and, as the bowler ran in, Audrey knew exactly where she'd hit the ball. Years of playing cricket with her father and brother made her good at the sport. She'd always been athletic, much to her mother's dismay, and now she grinned as she whacked the ball hard, hooking it over to the blanket where it landed just inches from Jake's feet.

Surprised, Valerie rose up on her knees. 'Audrey, are you *trying* to kill one of us?'

'Sorry, Val!' She laughed and got into position again. For the next eight balls she hit every one in their direction. Valerie had run for cover, but Jake still sat on the blanket, slowly clapping each ball she hit.

'I say, how splendid!' The colonel took out his handkerchief and wiped the sweat from his head and neck. 'I don't have to run at all.'

'Miss Pearson is too good for us.' Nielson chuckled as she hit another ball that sailed over his head.

'She should play for England!' Major Johnson winked at her and she winked back.

'Will you have a bowl, Captain Harding?' Price threw him the ball.

'No, I don't think so.' Jake glanced at Audrey.

'Frightened I might hit you for six, Captain?' she teased.

He stood and juggled the ball from hand to hand, his gaze not leaving hers. 'Not at all, Miss Pearson.'

Audrey swallowed, watching him walk to the bowler's mark. Her stomach twisted into knots at the challenge. After missing his first two balls, she realised he was very good at this game and was determined not to let her win this match between them. He had a steely look in his eyes, his expression grim.

She managed to hit his next delivery back over his head. Jake looked at her in surprise as the men whooped and clapped at the shot. 'Run Colonel! Run!' she called.

'Someone get that ball,' Jake yelled, raking his fingers through his hair in frustration. He glared at Audrey as she came to his end of the wicket.

'Don't take pity on me simply because I'm a woman, Captain.' She grinned at him and turned to stand at the side. 'I'm stronger than you know.'

The ball was thrown back to him, he caught it and then paused to examine the stitching. 'I don't doubt that for a moment, Miss Pearson.'

Inside, Audrey smiled. She was getting to him, unsettling his ordered life. She wasn't someone he could dismiss without another thought; she wouldn't let him.

With the next ball she hit it high and long. Major Johnson circled beneath it; hands outstretched. 'It's mine.'

'Run, Colonel,' Audrey yelled and took off down to the other end, while everyone screamed for Johnson to catch the ball.

Anxious, Jake ran in Johnson's direction. 'Don't drop it, don't drop it.'

Grinning, Johnson dived to catch the ball as it came down, only to miss it completely and land with a thud in the sand.

Howls of protests and laughter erupted. Jake swore and shook his head.

Audrey did a victory dance with the Colonel and then went up to hug Johnson. 'An excellent miss, Major, wonderfully done.' She brushed the sand off his shoulders.

Dusting off his trousers, Johnson winked. 'For you, Miss Pearson, anything.'

Amid the good-heated calls of favouritism and cheating, Audrey looked at Jake.

He scowled, turned away and tossed the ball to another player. Again, dismissing her. 'I need a drink.'

Then it came, the soft drone. As one, they all turned to look over the sea at the horizon. Like miniature toys, a swarm of planes headed towards them in a v formation. Behind them, from the village, the air raid siren wound out its alarm like a rising wail.

They were so weary of air raids, of disruption. The gaiety went out of them as they turned to gradually pack up the picnic. Mumbles and curses of a good day ruined accompanied the tidy up. With regret they packed away knowing the German planes wouldn't bomb them; they were after the larger industrial towns of York, Leeds and Manchester, it was only on their return home that they'd offload any left-over bombs along the coast. Still, the habit of the last four years was hard to dislodge and the fun, lazy day spirit was replaced with war-weariness.

Heart heavy, Audrey gathered the stumps and bat under her arm and headed towards the others, disappointed that her opportunity to be with Jake was cut short. Likely, he'd go back to his routine of forgetting her presence, of keeping his distance.

Nielson's hands shook as he helped tidy up. He'd started to fold the blanket, but soon was frozen with fear as the planes flew over, dappling the area with shade as they flew between them and the sun. Their engine noise drowned out any other sound.

'It's all right, Sid.' Audrey touched his arm and packed away the cricket gear.

Nielson suddenly dropped to the sand, screaming, the blanket pulled down over his head. Jake rushed to him as did the others, but he told them to go up to the house with Sister Lewis and Lucy and get into the cellar.

Only Audrey remained behind. She stood to the side, watching Jake coax and soothe Sid, who sat rocking, hugging his knees. 'We shouldn't stay down here, Captain. The tides turning.' She pointed to water, inching its way forward with every wave.

'You go up, I'll be fine here for a little while longer.' He ran his hand through his hair. 'I'll get him onto the cliff path in a moment. We'll be safe there.'

'I'll stay with you.'

'No, that's not necessary. I don't want to have to worry over you too.' He knelt beside Sid, dismissing her.

'I can look after myself, but you might need a hand with Sid.'

'No, I won't.'

'Jake-'

He waved her away, frowning, annoyed. 'Go on, go.'

'I'm not leaving you.'

'Christ, Audrey, will you do as I ask?' he snapped. 'I don't want you here.'

She raised her chin, refusing to let his words hurt. 'I want to help.'

'I don't need your help. I'm not your charity case, I'm not your anything! So, leave me alone.'

'Why? So you can wallow in self-pity?' Angry, she crossed her arms over her chest. 'Are you content to spend your life pushing people away, people who care?'

He jerked to his feet and grabbed her arms, his face white with rage. 'I never wanted you to care. I never asked for it! My life suited me until I came here, until you had to pry and believe you were what I needed. Well, I don't need you, Audrey Pearson, not now, not ever. Do you understand?'

She tore out of his grip, her heart thumping so much she thought it would leap out of her chest. 'I understand perfectly, Captain.' She was pleased her voice didn't shake. 'But there will come a day in your lonely life when you realise you've made a big mistake.' She glanced at Sid who had stopped rocking and was staring out to sea. 'Will your patients be enough to make you happy in the years to come?' On shaky legs she walked away.

Chapter Nine

Jake signed the form at his desk in the drawing room, feeling as though there was a lead weight pressing down on his chest. Since his unpleasant argument with Audrey on the beach, he'd toyed with the idea of leaving, being transferred elsewhere, and it would have made things simpler to do so, but he held back. His mind said that his work here was important, that men like Nielson were improving under his care. His heart disagreed and told him that he stayed for one reason only, Audrey.

Yet, he couldn't believe what his heart told him, didn't want to think that she affected him in any other way but as a beautiful woman who attracted him in a physical sense. He could deal with sexual yearning for it didn't need the heart to participate, but what he couldn't deal with was the notion of caring for someone again. He fell too deeply, loved beyond all reason. It wasn't healthy. It wasn't right that a man should be so devoted to a woman. Surely that was a sign of weakness? His mother always said he was too passionate and caring, that he'd never make it as a doctor because he'd feel too much for his patients' suffering. She was correct to a certain degree. He'd let his emotions rule him too many times in both his career and his private life.

He had loved not only Marianne too much, but the whole family scenario, and it had cost him dearly when she and the baby died. When his dreams of becoming a father, something he had wanted so very much, were shattered, he believed his life was over, had even tried to make it so. Never again did he want to be at such a point in his life. And he knew that if he fell in love with Audrey, he would once more be totally devoted, and therefore completely open to those horrendous depths of pain for a second time. He wouldn't put himself through that again.

Sighing deeply, he rubbed the tiredness from his eyes. With another flourish of his pen, he signed that Colonel Barnes was fit for office duty, that Major Johnson was fit to return to his unit, that Lieutenants Price, Evans and Pope were fit to return to their units, and also Sergeant Hughes. He couldn't help but feel he had signed these men's death warrants: that his signature was sending them back into battle to be shot at, to live with death once more.

The sound of wheels crunching on the drive made him look out the tall window. A fellow on a bicycle rode to a stop and placed the bike by the house wall.

From the hall came footsteps, talking, and then through the open drawing room door, Jake watched Audrey and Valerie greet the messenger as he came through the front door.

'Robert, how nice to see you.' Valerie smiled. 'What do you have for us this time?'

'A few things, Sister Lewis.' He pulled from his satchel several envelopes and handed them over. 'I'm also paying a social call.' The young man grinned, his gaze straying to Audrey.

Jake felt the weight press further onto his chest. That young pup was making eyes at Audrey. Fascinated, he leant forward, placing his elbows on the desk, studying them. Audrey laughed, a light tinkling laugh at something the other man whispered. Jake clenched his jaw, making himself remain in the chair, when instinct told him to get up and make his presence known to Audrey. He wanted her to laugh with him not that young puppy, but then he hardly gave her reason to even smile at him. What had possessed him to speak so harshly to her, to throw her affection back in her face like that?

'Please excuse me, I've paperwork waiting for me.' Valerie left them and stepped into the drawing room, giving Jake a smile. 'How's it all going?'

'Nearly done.' He moved in the chair so he could see past Valerie and into the hall, but it was now empty.

'There's mail for you too.' Valerie placed two brown envelopes on his desk.

Ignoring them, Jake stood, went to the window and stared at Audrey and the Robert fellow standing out on the drive. He detested the younger man for being so…*free*. He doubted Robert had dreams of his wife bleeding to death, or the images of his baby lying blue and lifeless on a sheet.

'Do you need Robert to take something into town for you?' Valerie asked, coming to stand beside him as she opened her post.

'No.' Jake clenched his fists as the man took Audrey's hand and kissed it like some gallant knight.

'What's this fellow playing at? I'm sure Miss Pearson has more important things to do than to pass the time of day with a messenger.'

'Audrey doesn't look in any hurry to get back to work, by the looks of it.' Valerie chuckled, gave him a knowing grin and returned to her desk. 'Still, who can blame her for wanting a good-looking man's attention? Life can be so dreary at times.'

'Is that what she wants from a man, just attention?' Was Audrey so superficial? Could she not really care for him as she made out she did? If so, then he'd no need to feel so guilty for rejecting her.

Valerie laughed. 'No, poor Audrey, she wants it all, marriage, babies, a man to sweep her off her feet.' The amusement left her as she sat down. 'I hope she gets it one day, and the man who she gives her love to will be extremely lucky, for she has it in abundance.'

Jake turned away from the window, his mind in turmoil. He met Valerie's gaze and he realised that she knew about him and Audrey, such as they were. 'Don't look to me to fill that role.'

'Why ever not?' Val frowned. 'You must be aware she has fallen in love with you?'

'Not so much that it's stopping her from flirting with messenger boy out there.' He waved towards the window.

'That means nothing, and you know it.'

'Well, perhaps she should try harder with him and forget her intentions about me. I'm not the one for her.'

'You seem very decided about that. Why?'

Jake groaned. This was fast spinning out of control. 'Because I don't want a relationship. I don't want-'

'To feel?' Val smiled sadly. 'I know all about that, Captain.'

'No, you don't, not like I do.' He played with a letter opener on his desk, wondering why on earth he was talking like this with Sister Lewis. He never spoke to staff of his private life.

Valerie got up and poured them a brandy from the medicine cabinet in the corner and then shut the drawing room door. 'I want to tell you something about my past which will show you I do understand perfectly.'

~ ~ ~

Audrey left the cloakroom and headed for the hall, yawning widely as she did so. She'd spent the entire day in the vegetable gardens, digging out weeds and spreading compost. Her back pained from bending over for hours and her feet hurt from standing up all day. She longed for a hot bath and a cup of tea.

Hearing the sound of furniture being moved, she paused outside the dining room door and listened. Scraping sounded on the wooden floorboards along with Lucy's laughter.

'What is she up to?' Audrey whispered and opened the door.

Lucy stood poised mid action of moving a small table. 'Oh, there you are. I was about to come find you.'

'What are you doing?' Audrey looked around the room. The table and chairs were pushed to one side and Lieutenant Price stood by the window red-faced.

'Setting it up for some dancing.' Lucy lifted the radio onto the table and fiddled with the knobs on it. 'There's a special two-hour dancing session on the wireless. It starts in a few minutes. I thought we could have a night of dancing. It's only waltzing and the like, no jitterbugging I shouldn't think, but it's better than nothing and free.'

'The men—'

'Oh, they'll be down in a minute.' Lucy turned to Price. 'Do pull down the blackouts, Pricy-boy, there's a good chap.'

Behind Audrey, the door opened, and Val and Mrs Graham entered carrying trays of food and drinks. Audrey blinked in surprise. 'You knew about this too?'

Valerie frowned placing the tray on the dining table. 'Of course, why wouldn't we?' Then she looked over at Lucy. 'You did mention it to Audrey, didn't you?'

Lucy shrugged and tossed her hair with a flick of her head. 'I'm sure I did...'

Annoyed, Audrey crossed her arms over her chest. 'No, you didn't, Lucy. You didn't tell me because you knew I would have said no.'

'Oh, *Lucy*,' Val tutted. 'You said Audrey was fine about it.'

Mrs Graham scuttled out of the room, while Price and Val stood awkwardly by the window.

Adjusting the volume of the radio, Lucy ignored them while an announcer spoke of the music line up for the night.

Audrey let her anger build. 'I won't have you behaving as though we didn't bury our father only weeks ago. It's disrespectful.'

'Nonsense. Father would want us to be happy. I thought we could have a night of dancing because most of the officers will be leaving us soon. It's a send-off for them.'

'Turn the music off, Lucy. You're not doing this.'

116

Lucy gave her a defiant stare. 'It's all been ar-ranged.'

'Then unarranged it!' Audrey stormed over to the wireless and switched it off.

'No, I shan't.' A steely look came into Lucy's eyes. 'I want some fun. I'm sick of being surrounded by dreary people and this dreary war.'

'Don't be so selfish,' Audrey snapped. 'You're not a child to demand a party when it suits you. I can't believe you went behind my back to organise this.'

'You're such a stick in the mud, that's why. *We can't do this! We can't do that!*' Lucy mimicked, hands on hips. 'I've had enough of it. You're not my mother and this is my house too.'

Val took a step forward and opened her mouth to speak, but at the same time the door opened again, and the officers sauntered in talking and joking.

Lucy smiled at them. 'Good, you're all here. I've got a few girls coming from the village that I know, to even up the numbers.' She swivelled back to the table and switched the music on. 'There's plenty of drinks and food. We'll have a wonderful night.'

'I'm going for a bath.' Audrey spun on her heel and left the room. In the hallway Valerie caught up with her.

'I'm sorry, Aud, I didn't know.'

'It's not your fault. Lucy is to blame. I cannot be-lieve her behaviour. To be so sneaky. It's not like her.'

There was a knock at the front door and Valerie went down the hall to open it. Three young men and two giggling teenage girls stood on the doorstep hold-ing bottles of wine.

'How do!' One fellow crowed, his hat low over his eyes and an arm around the girl next to him. He was good looking with a deep tan and flashed a bright smile. 'We heard there was a party on tonight.'

They swarmed into the house, laughing and calling Lucy's name as Valerie showed them to the dining room. She returned frowning. 'I think they were drunk.'

'I don't even know them.' Audrey mounted the stairs. 'Lucy will get a tongue lashing in the morning.'

Val hesitated. 'Shouldn't we go and keep an eye on them?'

Conscious of her aches and another long day of working in the garden tomorrow, Audrey shook her head. 'I need a bath and sleep. Lucy thinks she's adult enough to handle it, so let her.'

'I guess the officers will keep an eye on things.' Val checked her watch. 'Captain Harding will be home in a few hours.'

'Oh?' Audrey tried to show no interest, but she hadn't known he was gone from the house. On purpose she rose early and stayed out in the grounds with Owen and Alf all day. Avoiding the Captain was becoming one of her talents.

'Yes, he went to Hull this morning. There is a doctor up from London who is holding a lecture on treating soldiers with problems of the mind. The Captain has been talking about it all week.'

Irrationally, Audrey felt shut out, and also jealous of Valerie. Captain Harding had been freely talking with Val, but he never did it with her. In fact, he went out his way to avoid being in her presence. This week, she had tried to give him some of his own treatment. Only to find that it backfired on her, because she didn't know his thoughts, or what he talked about or where he was going. To shun him had left her in the dark even more than normal. She was a fool. She'd given him exactly what he wanted. But what was the alternative, more rejection?

Depressed, she went up a few more steps before Val caught her attention again. 'Yes?'

A soft look of worry crossed Val's face. 'Don't give up on him Audrey. He's a good man and worth the effort.'

'He's not interested in me, Val. He doesn't seek me out, doesn't smile in my direction.'

'There are reasons, I'm sure. He's suffered—'

'I know his past, his pain. I've tried to show him I understand, but he's not willing to take a chance on love, on me.'

'Give him time.'

'I would, willingly, if he gave me a hint that time was all he needed.'

'Audrey, he's one of those men who don't wear their heart on their sleeve. He's not going to show his feelings or even admit to them until he's sure.'

'So, in the meantime I'm meant to keep humiliating myself? Do you know how many times he's rejected my friendship, my caring? I don't know if I can keep putting myself through it, in fact I know I can't keep doing it.' She smiled sadly down at her friend, tears blurring her vision. 'I may have feelings for him, but I can't make *him* feel for *me*.' With that she hurried up the staircase and into her room.

~ ~ ~

Jake opened the front door to music and howls of laughter coming from down the hall. He stepped inside and automatically looked into the drawing room, his and Sister Lewis's office, for sometimes Audrey sat in there to keep Valerie company. He ignored the pang of disappointment when he saw only Valerie at her desk with the lamp on, writing notes.

She looked up as he entered the room. 'Oh, you're back. How did it go?'

'Fine.' He placed his case by the door, went to his desk and picked up his mail. As always, he half listened for the presence of Audrey. On the train coming back from Hull all he'd done was think of her — even his medical reading material hadn't engrossed him as it normally did. All this fantasising about her had to stop. It wasn't healthy and was slowly driving him mad. To save his sanity, he had to harden his heart and mind to her. The tender looks she gave him must no longer affect him if he was to continue working here, but then that may soon be changing and none of it would matter anymore...

'A long day?' Valerie smiled in sympathy.

'Too long, but interesting and worth it.' He rolled his neck, stretching out the aches there and in his shoulders. Music and singing filled the normally quiet house. 'Have I missed a party?'

Valerie raised her eyebrows and set down her pencil. 'Lucy. It was meant to be a few hours of dancing to the radio, or so she said, but she invited other people and apparently word got around quick, because people have been arriving for hours. It has grown into a nightmare. The dining room is littered with drunken strangers and,' she paused and grimaced, 'I'm afraid we have drunk patients too.'

Sighing, Jake threw his mail back on the desk. 'That's all we need.'

'That's not the worst of it.'

'Oh?'

'Lucy went behind Audrey's back about it all and Audrey's non too happy to say the least. She feels it's too soon after their father passing away. The atmosphere in the morning may not be pleasant.'

'We forget that this is their home, they are a family, and all the concerns that go with it.'

'Yes, that's true.' Valerie yawned behind her hand. 'Are you off duty soon?'

'Not for a few hours, not that there's much to do now. Without the house full of sick men, I feel a bit of a fraud. There's isn't a lot I can do for patients who aren't physically ill.'

'Nonsense. You're work here is terribly important. The men are still ill, it is just mental not physically. I can't be here on my own, now can I?'

'Yes, I know that, but I feel as though things are changing here somehow…'

Jake crossed his arms and leant against the desk. 'You want to work in a hospital again?'

Valerie toyed with her pencil. 'I suppose I do. I'm not occupied here enough, and it makes me think too much.'

'I understand that.'

'But to leave Audrey and Lucy is like leaving my family and I feel disloyal by wanting to go.'

A bang and the sound of smashing glass filtered through to them. Jake swore under his breath. 'I think we've all had enough for one night, yes?' He looked at Valerie.

'Absolutely. It's past eleven. I have no idea how the others are getting home.'

'Let's get the guests out the door and the patients into bed.'

Valerie joined him at the door and then stepped into the hall. 'Yes, before Audrey is made more upset than she already is.'

'A little late for that I think.' Audrey stood at the top of the stairs, fastening her dressing gown belt tighter around her waist.

Jake swore under his breath as his heart hammered against his chest at the sight of her. She was too lovely for his peace of mind, too good for him altogether. Living here with her made each day harder and harder for him to stop thinking about her. He struggled now to think of a life without her. Within a few months she'd crept into his heart and seemed firmly lodged there, but it wouldn't do. He couldn't, wouldn't love again.

'Go back up to bed, Aud. We'll handle it.' Valerie offered.

'Coming down the stairs, Audrey shook her head, her eyes glinting with anger. 'No. It's my home, *my sister*. She's had her fun, now I'm going to put a stop to it.' She gave Jake a fleeting glance before striding down to the dining room.

Jake looked at Valerie, who shrugged her shoulders, and they both followed.

At the door, he stood and after quickly scanning his patients to ascertain their state, he watched Audrey stride through the gathering to the radio. With a flick of her wrist the music had gone, and she turned to glare at Lucy, who knelt by the table picking up pieces of a broken plate. 'The party *is* over.'

Lucy nodded and bowed her head so that her curls fell and hid her burning face.

'Who is this tasty morsel of a woman before me?' A tall, thin man dressed in a navy suit stepped out of a circle of people. Jake guessed him to be about thirty.

Lucy straightened, her face pale. 'Audrey, please—'

Audrey held up her hand to silence Lucy and gave the fellow a condescending look. 'Who I am is no concern of yours. All you need to be concerned about is that the party has finished, and you are all going home.'

'Let me introduce myself.' He smiled and bowed like a gallant knight. 'I'm Ralph Dolton. Perhaps we can have a drink together?' His eyes roamed over her leisurely, lingering where her dressing gown crossed over her breasts.

Jake took a step away from the door, angered by the man's rudeness. 'I suggest you listen to Miss Pearson, Dolton.'

Dolton flicked him a dismissing hand and leaned closer to whisper in Audrey's ear. Her eyes widened in surprise at his murmuring and it was enough to send the blood rushing to Jake's head. He lunged forward, gripped Dolton's shoulders and flung him towards the door. 'Get away from her!'

Jake turned when someone tapped him on the back. He had no time to react before the fist crashed into his nose, knocking him backwards against some-one else. Stars burst in front of his eyes. The pain ricocheted around his head. A scream joined the general noise of yelling and shouting, and then the next moment he was grabbed again and thumped in the stomach. With a groan, he doubled up and fell to his knees. His mind couldn't understand the chaos around him as it fought to control the pain in different parts of his body.

The room erupted into a squabbling mess of bodies and noise. Gingerly, Jake stood, only to be knocked sideways when two men, Price being one of them, crashed into him. Wildly he looked for Audrey, but in the craziness, he couldn't see her. To the side of the room, Valerie leant over two young women, protecting them from the mayhem as she dabbed at bloodied noses and lips.

Blood dripped from his nose. Fury overrode his pain, as he saw Dolton edge his way towards the door. Cowardly bastard! Forgetting everything but the need of revenge, Jake pushed his way through the brawling, grabbed Dolton's arm and swung him around. He instinctively punched him hard on the jaw. *God Almighty!* For an instant he couldn't believe the intense pain that shot up his hand, but the sight of Dolton falling over onto his backside helped eased it.

Jake spun and faced the room, waiting for the next one to come at him.

A gunshot blasted, the sound so loud Jake jumped and twisted back to the door. A girl screamed then fainted. He stared in amazement at Audrey, who stood in the doorway pointing her father's gun up to the ceiling.

'You wouldn't listen the first time, so perhaps you'll listen now.' Her green eyes narrowed and scanned the room, a look of hate on her face. 'Unless you sleep under this roof, you will leave immediately or wear the next bullet.'

Jake blinked, not able to take his gaze off her. Her black curls sprang wild about her head and her stance was one that brooked no argument.

Dolton scrambled to his feet, wiping the blood from a cut lip and nodded to his cohorts. Together they sidled past Audrey with Dolton being the last to leave. He lingered, a grin playing about his lips. 'It was a pleasure, Miss Pearson. It's not every day one is threatened with a gun on *this* side of the channel.'

'Then perhaps you should think about joining up and experiencing it for real.'

'Medical reasons, my dear,' he laughed, 'medical reasons.'

Audrey raised an eyebrow at him. 'Real or imaginary?'

His laughter rang throughout the hallway as he sauntered away.

Jake let out a breath. The bastard needed a good kicking.

The officers, amazingly sober now, started to put the room to rights. Only Jake kept still, watching Audrey's face, seeing the subtle signs of hidden distress.

'No, stop, all of you.' Audrey held up a hand, her stance rigid. 'Leave it. Just go.'

'Miss Pearson, let us fix the room again.' Major Johnson righted a chair.

'I said to go, now!'

Unsettled by her cold demand, the men hurried from the room. The village girls quickly followed them, leaving Lucy, Valerie, Audrey and himself in the shattered remains of the dining room. Jake's heart clamped at the steeliness of Audrey's manner. She looked brittle, ready to break or go mad at the slightest touch.

'Audrey,' Lucy whispered, tears filling her eyes. 'I'm sorry, so sorry.'

'Get out of my sight, Lucy.' Audrey didn't even look at her sister as Lucy slipped past her and ran down the hallway crying. Audrey placed the gun by the wall, her movements jerky.

'Well, this won't do.' Valerie tucked away her bloodied handkerchief she'd used to clean up someone's face. 'Poor Mrs Graham will have a fit in the morning seeing this mess.' Efficiently as always, she found a tray beneath the table and started stacking cups and plates onto it.

Jake looked at Audrey, who seemed rooted to the spot. Treating her like one of his patients, he pretended not to notice her unless she gave him encouragement to do so. Broken glass surrounded him, and he knelt to pick it up.

Piece by piece he dropped the glass into an ice bucket, aware of Audrey silently moving around the room, straightening chairs, collecting glasses, stubbing out half lit cigarettes, doing whatever came to hand. Valerie went in and out of the room emptying trays. They worked in silence for about fifteen minutes and he covertly watched Audrey, checking her movements, watching for some sign that she might need him.

Valerie came in minus the tray and instead carried a broom. 'I'll sweep the floor while the cups and plates soak in the sink.'

'I'll wash up, Val,' Audrey whispered, leaving the room.

He paused in taking off the tablecloth and looked at Valerie. 'I don't like the look of her.'

'No, neither do I. Her colour isn't good, all grey and pasty.'

'Shock.'

'That whole thing with the gun. It scared me. I've never seen her behave like that. It's out of character.'

'I think it is a culmination of a lot of events happening so close. She feels out of control. Even those who don't fight in battles, still can suffer the effects of war and its consequences.'

Valerie nodded. 'Go and help her. I'll finish in here and then up and check on the men. Stay with her.'

'I don't think I'm the right person for that. Her feelings towards me haven't helped the situation.'

'And you don't love her.' Valerie stated sadly.

'I wish it was as easy as that.' He truly did. To not love her would make his life much smoother, but he had the sinking feeling it was too late, and that Audrey Pearson meant a lot to him.

Taking a deep breath, he left and walked down to the kitchen. At the door he hesitated, mentally preparing himself to be helpful, to be in the role of a doctor, to keep his feelings squashed.

She turned as he opened the door and went down the steps. Her gaze lingered on him a second before she once more concentrated on washing the dishes.

'I've come to help.' He smiled, wanting to lighten to atmosphere, to make her feel at ease.

'Thank you. Does your nose hurt?'

He tapped it gingerly. 'I'll live.'

'I'm sorry you got hurt in all that.'

'It got out of hand. It happens.'

'I don't understand Lucy anymore. Since Father died, she's changed.'

'She's also growing up.'

'Yes.' She sighed deeply; her shoulders bowed.

Side by side they worked without speaking. What she washed, he dried and stacked. 'I used to help my mother wash up after Sunday dinner. She never left me help any other day but Sunday.' He smiled, remembering.

'Until the war, I had never washed up. Didn't need to, as we had staff. But they left to work in the munitions factories or joined up.'

'You never wanted to join up?'

'I thought about it, but Mother was sick and then died, then Robbie went to war and was killed the following year. It was too much for Father, he needed Lucy and I to be home, and then the soldiers arrived, and I had enough work to do here, as Father was too frail to cope, especially when the staff number reduced.'

'Did you resent having to stay here?' He encouraged her to talk, finding it a great way of helping someone to think things through in their own way.

'No, not at all. I love my home and this area. We have been so busy here in the last few years that I never had time to miss something I knew nothing about.'

Silence stretched between them, a comfortable silence that was restful and healing.

Audrey let her hands hang in the soapy water. 'I'm sorry.'

Jake paused in putting a plate on the table. 'For what?'

'Tonight and…and before…the frankness. I should never have told you I loved you.'

'You don't have to be sorry for any of that. They drove you to be angry. Lucy showed no respect by having that party and inviting strangers you didn't approve of.' He stood close beside her, his stomach twisting with compassion. 'As for you loving me, or thinking you're in love with me, well, we cannot control our hearts. I am terribly honoured.'

She slowly turned and faced him. Her green eyes grew soft with tears. She lightly touched her wet fingertips to his face and his groin contracted with a familiar ache of want. He felt himself weaken with every stroke of her fingers across his cheek, jaw and down his neck. Swallowing became difficult and he sucked in a breath. With a light tenderness only a woman could give, she rubbed one finger over his lips, and he flicked out his tongue to touch it.

'Kiss me,' she whispered, her tone deep and filled with longing.

Every ounce of him wanted to, he throbbed to pull her close and give into the lust that burned in his blood. Yet, it would only confuse them more. He wouldn't dig another hole for himself, not when he was leaving…

He caught her hands and lowered them to her side. 'We mustn't.'

Audrey's head fell forward, covering her blush. She laughed harshly. 'No, of course not. To kiss me would bring the sky down on our heads or cause the world to end!'

He cringed at her sarcasm. 'Audrey—'

'Go away, Jake, please.'

The sorrow in her voice broke his heart and the pain he had never wanted to experience again — the pain he'd done his best to avoid — came back to rip at his chest once more. Yes, he would go away, as he'd planned to do today while on the train.

Chapter Ten

Audrey moved her knight on the chessboard and took a sip of wine.

Grinning, Lucy swiped one of her pawns. 'This is too easy.'

'You know I don't play well, not like Father and Robbie could.'

'You're not concentrating.' Lucy sipped her own wine and took a piece of cheese from the plate. They were sitting in the kitchen, the house quieter than ever for they'd not received new replacements after the departure of Colonel Barnes, Major Johnson, Lieutenant Price, Sergeant Hughes and several other officers, plus two of the nurses.

The August heat easily sapped their energy, and although it was late, the summer warmth had barely lessened after the sun went down.

'I don't feel in the mood.' Audrey yawned, her muscles aching. She'd been toiling in the vegetable garden all day, using hard work as a tool to forget about Jake. Her plan to make him fall in love with her had failed dismally, and instead all she'd received was hurt and rejection. She'd offered affection to him and he didn't want it. She felt a fool. How could she have believed he would love her? She was nothing special.

'We should have gone to the dance.'

Audrey shivered, remembering the last dance she attended, and of being in Jake's arms. 'It's too hot to dance. That hall would be like an oven.'

'Well, it's better than staying home all the time being terribly bored.'

'Only *you* get bored, Lucy. Besides after the last dancing episode you organised, I'd rather not talk about anything concerning dancing.'

Lucy scowled. 'Why did you have to bring that up again? I have apologised over and over for nearly two weeks. It's forgotten. Please don't speak of it again.'

'Sometimes sorry isn't enough, Lucy.'

'What more do you want? I said I'd learnt my lesson.'

'Then why does that Ralph Dolton keep calling you on the telephone? Tell him to stay away.'

'He has telephoned once!'

Audrey gulped her wine, fed up with her wishes being ignored. 'I won't have him here again. I mean it. I have forgiven you about the party, but don't push it too far, I'm telling you.'

'I'm not a child.'

'Then don't act like one. We don't know that Dolton fellow.'

Lucy banged her hand on the table. '*I* know him. He's my friend! Why can't you give him a chance?'

'Because he has to be thirty or more, too old for you, and he's too smarmy—'

'Smarmy? How can you know? You met him once when we'd all had too much to drink. How can you judge him when you behaved so despicably yourself?'

The door opened and Valerie came down the step. 'There you two are. I could hear you down the hall.'

'Sorry about that.' Audrey gave Lucy a quelling look. 'The heat has made us bad tempered. Are you off duty now?' she asked, rising to get her a glass of wine.

'Yes, thankfully. My feet ache, though I don't know why, we aren't that busy now.' She smiled her thanks as Audrey passed her the wineglass. 'Though the paperwork never seems to stop.'

'Will we get more men?'

Val shrugged. 'Not sure. No news yet.' She looked at the wine. 'Are we celebrating something?'

Audrey refilled her own glass. 'Yes. It is our mother's birthday today. Father always opened a bottle of his most expensive wine, usually hidden in the cellar, to celebrate her day. We thought we'd keep the tradition going.'

'Only we don't have an elaborate dinner to go with it, which is disappointing.' Lucy scowled.

'A toast then.' Val raised her glass and they joined her. 'Happy birthday to the very much loved and sorely missed Joanna Pearson.'

'Happy birthday, Mother,' Audrey and Lucy chorused.

Just then the door opened again, and Jake entered. 'I wondered where you'd all got to. The house seems too big and quiet now it's nearly empty.'

'I was thinking the same, Captain.' Valerie poured him the last of the wine.

'You must play chess with me, Captain,' Lucy said. 'Audrey is totally dreadful.'

'Very well, but I warn you I'm rather good at it. I played against my father for many years and he was an excellent player.' He smiled and Audrey had to turn away. His mere presence sent her heart into a twirl. In the last week he'd not been so distant and had tried to forge some kind of friendship between them again, but this time she'd held back. She didn't want just friendship. He hurt her too easily with his harsh words and hot and cold manner. When he was being kind and considerate, her love blossomed, overwhelming her in its intensity, but she knew how quickly he turned again into someone morose and remote.

As Lucy set up the board again, she pointed to the letter Valerie held. 'What do you have there?'

'It seems I'm going away.' Valerie tried to look happy but failed miserably. The paper in her hand shook. 'Unfortunately, the army nurse corps has remembered me, and that I have a lovely home here. They obviously feel that I should be somewhere less comfortable.'

'But why now?' Audrey whispered, the blood draining from her face.

'You know it was only a temporary arrangement to begin with, Aud.' Val smiled. 'We were lucky that I slipped through the cracks and was allowed to stay on here as long as I have.'

'Where will they send you?'

'I'm joining a replacement unit that's heading for Normandy.'

'France?' Lucy's eyes widened, shock holding her rigid. 'But the newspapers report that the Germans are on the run. The Americans have captured St Lo. They say Paris is in their sights.'

'I don't understand why they are sending you now? It makes no sense to me.' Audrey murmured, believing that Val wasn't as shocked about this abrupt news as she should be. 'You won't be coming back, will you?'

Valerie shook her head. 'No, I shouldn't think so, not until after the war. I'll come back and see you then.'

Audrey put her hand to her throat, sadness seeping into every pore.

Valerie stood and hugged her. 'It's my time, Audrey. I don't mind, really. Those nurses on the front line deserve a break. In fact, I'm glad I'm going.'

'You're glad?' Lucy gaped, astonished.

'Yes. Other nurses, closer to the battle fronts have had to do their job in terrible conditions, under fire. Why should I be spared from it?'

'But-'

'There is no but, dearest. It has been decided and I'll follow my orders like all the others have done before me.' Valerie unfolded the letter and then folded it again.

Suspicious, Audrey drew a quick breath. 'You asked for it, didn't you? You requested the transfer. The truth now.'

Her cheeks reddening, Val nodded. 'Yes, I did. I had to.'

'Why?' Audrey whispered, ignoring Lucy's intake of breath.

'I'm not needed here anymore.' Val glanced at Jake. 'And I couldn't live with myself if I didn't do my bit in the war.'

Audrey stood so fast her chair rocked. 'You have done your bit! How can you say otherwise? What we've done here isn't nothing.'

'I know, dearest, I know.'

Jake cleared his throat. 'Perhaps Valerie wants to do her share at the field hospitals and make herself available for promotion.'

'Promotion?' Audrey glared at him in confusion and then at Val. 'Is this true?'

Val fiddled with the letter in her hand but held her chin high. 'Partly, yes. Nursing is my career. Being tucked away in the country won't see me rise in superiority.'

Audrey blinked, finding it difficult to take in. 'This is so important to you that you'd put yourself in danger?'

'Of course. I must, as others have done also.' Val shrugged as though it wasn't an issue. 'Captain Harding understands.'

'When do you leave?' Audrey murmured; her heart full.

Stuffing the letter back into the envelope, Valerie glanced up at them. 'Tomorrow.'

'So soon? How long have you known?' Audrey glanced wildly from Valerie to Lucy to Jake. She desperately wanted him to hold her, but he wouldn't, and she couldn't rely on him for the kind of comfort she badly needed.

'Since this morning.'

'Why didn't you say something earlier,' Lucy begged, tears spilling over her lashes.

'I didn't want a fuss, dearest.' Valerie reached across and gripped Lucy's hand. 'This is going to be hard enough without you being upset. So, stop your tears.'

Jake stood; the chess game forgotten. 'Sister Lewis isn't the only nurse to leave. Nurse Nugent and Williams will be going with her. I've been informed that there won't be another intake of patients for some time, if at all.'

Audrey stared at him. Everything was changing, shifting like sand to make her unstable in her own home.

Val straightened. 'I need to speak with the other nurses and then pack.' She looked at Jake, becoming business-like. 'Nurse Jones will be the senior nurse once I'm gone, Captain Harding. Nurse Proctor is very reliable but may need some guidance as she continues her training.'

He smiled reassuringly. 'I'll take care of them.'

Valerie nodded and glanced at Lucy, who sobbed quietly into a handkerchief. 'Don't cry, Lucy, I beg you. This is hard enough as it is.' She paused by Audrey to grip her shoulder for a moment before walking out of the room.

'This is *just* awful!' Lucy ran from the room in tears.

Silence filled the room and Audrey shivered. In the space of ten minutes everything had altered. All that had been normal for the last few years gone.

Jake fiddled with a chess piece. 'She'll be fine in France. Nurses are-'

'Please don't speak, Captain Harding.' Audrey gave him a withering glare. 'Nothing you can say will help. Valerie is like a sister to Lucy and me and she's going off to war. Keep your words of comfort for your patients.'

'I'm simply-'

'Simply what, Captain?' she snapped, hating him for not loving her as she wanted, for not wrapping his arms around her and driving the world away.

'I'm trying to be your friend.'

'I don't want or need your friendship, Captain. I already have plenty of friends.'

He spread his arms out hopelessly. 'It's all I can offer.'

'No, it's all you *think* you can offer because you're a coward. You're too frightened to live your life again!' She spun on her heel and ran from the room.

Chapter Eleven

Audrey stood on the train platform amid the noise and the bustle of soldiers, civilians and transport assistants. The engine hisses steam and she scowled as coal smuts landed on her white gloves and duck-egg blue suit. She watched young soldiers hugging goodbye to families, seasoned soldiers kissing sweethearts and old businessmen twisting between them all to find their first-class carriage.

Her own throat was tight from tears, but she smiled as Valerie returned from putting her bag inside the train. 'All set?'

'Yes. Got my seat by the window.' Valerie held up her ticket. 'Though it's crowded already, so I put my basket on the seat and asked a young woman to mind it for me.'

'Don't forget to eat those sandwiches, Mrs Graham packed for you, you know how the trains are sometimes. You could be stopped for hours along the line.'

'Pray that doesn't happen.' Valerie grinned.

'And there's cake too that Lucy baked for you.'

'I don't think I can eat anything after our lunch.' She laughed.

Audrey chuckled. 'Lord, yes. I've not eaten like that for a long time.'

Valerie linked her arm through Audrey's. 'Well, it was a special treat, just you and me on our last day.'

Audrey's throat constricted. 'There will be other days. Promise me you'll come back to us when this madness is over.'

'Naturally, I will. I think of you as family now. Besides, after the war, when I'm working twelve-hour shifts in some cold dreary hospital, coming here for a break will be something to look forward to.'

'After the war is over, please try to get a post to a hospital nearby and not down south.'

'I'll do my best.'

They were jostled a bit from a group of soldiers lumping their kits bags without enthusiasm towards the train doors. The platform grew more crowded as the leaving time drew near.

Suddenly Audrey gripped Valerie's gloved hands. 'I don't want you to go, it'll not be the same without you.'

Tears gathered in Val's eyes. 'I know, but I must. Leaving you is hard for me too.'

'I feel I've wasted time. All those occasions when I should have spent more time with you, to learn more about you.'

'Don't be silly, Aud. We've lived together for over two years. We both have had important work to do, but our time together has been special, never wasted.'

'*You* had important work. I'm a fraud.'

'Nonsense,' Val barked. 'You give tired, hurt soldiers a home, a place to rest before they go back into

the lunacy that is war. You must never think what you
do is unworthy.'

'But I'll not be facing the same dangers you will
be.'

'We all have roles to play, and they are all signifi-
cant.' Val tilted her head to one side. 'And besides,
you know nearly everything there is to know about
me.'

'I do?' Audrey raised her eyebrows. 'I don't believe that for a minute.'

'Yes, well, not all…' Val looked down at her
shoes—sturdy, ugly brown nurse's shoes. 'I had a baby. Somewhere out there is a little boy who looks like
me.'

Audrey stared open mouthed. 'A baby? You-
you…but I-'

'Giving him away was the price I paid for love
when I was seventeen.'

'Oh, Val.'

Shaking her head, Val raised a timid smile. 'Don't
be sorry for me. I can do that job better than anyone.'

'Why didn't you tell me before now?'

'It was so long ago. He'd be seven now.'

'I wish you had told me before.'

'I can't live in the past, and I told Captain Harding
not to either.'

Audrey blinked. 'Captain Harding?'

'He's let his past, his loss blind him to any kind of
future happiness. I know how that can feel, but to be
normal, or as normal as possible, you have to allow
the past to recede or it'll eat away you, like it's doing
to him.'

The whistle blew making them jump. Valerie
threw her arms around Audrey. 'I love you like a sister.'

'Write all the time, about everything. I want to know it all, the good and bad.'

'I will, I promise. You must do so, too. I want to know how everyone is doing here. Send food tins when you can. Out there, the food is not so good, or so I've heard.'

'Don't worry, you'll get a parcel twice a month.' Audrey held her tight. 'Promise you'll come back to us after this is all over, promise.'

'I promise.' Valerie kissed her cheek and then straightened, once more becoming the competent nursing sister. 'Take care.'

'And you!' Audrey smiled as they parted.

At the door, Valerie showed her ticket to the stationmaster and then stepped inside. Audrey watched her find her seat and then the Valerie slid open the window and leaned out to grasp Audrey's hand. 'I'm glad I arrived at Twelve Pines because I gain two more sisters.'

Swallowing back tears, she kissed Val's hand. 'Twelve Pines will always be your home.'

'After the war...' Val paused as the whistle blew again and the engine hissed steam.

'Yes, after the war.'

'Oh, and Audrey?'

'Yes?'

'Don't give up on Captain Harding. He needs you.' Valerie smiled and ducked back inside the carriage as the train gathered speed. With a last wave she closed the window and turned away.

Audrey stood watching the train rattle away from the station. Steam shot out of the engine sides like snorts of smoke from a dragon. She felt hollow inside, alone and cold. It seemed she had spent the latter part of her life so far saying goodbye to people. One day she'd say goodbye to Lucy too no doubt, and then she'd truly be by herself.

She didn't know how long she stood on the platform, but gradually it all became quiet, the footsteps and murmurs faded away.

'She's gone?'

Audrey closed her eyes at Jake's voice and didn't look at him as he came to stand beside her. The fluttering in her stomach did nothing to help her sadness. She was tired of yearning for a man she couldn't have. Her nose twitched as tears gathered hot behind her eyes again.

'Nothing stays the same, does it?' He sighed.

'No.' Audrey turned and noticed how smart he looked today in full uniform with his cap set at a rakish angle. 'How-how did you get into town?'

He held out his arm for her. 'Got a lift with some farmer, luckily. I didn't fancy walking all the way.'

They strolled down the platform with Audrey keenly aware of his lithe body alongside hers. 'Why didn't you mention you wanted to come into town this morning? You could have come with us.'

He gave her a wry smile. 'I thought you all might want some time alone. I knew you and Lucy had planned to have lunch with Sister Lewis before she left.'

'Well, you still could have travelled in the car with us.'

Nearing the car, Audrey fished in her bag for the keys, conscious of him watching her. 'Lucy has arranged to go to watch a film with a friend and stay the night with her. She's coming home tomorrow. Do you want to travel back with me?'

'Actually, I thought we could go for a cup of tea.'

She paused her searching to stare at him. 'Tea? You want to have tea with me?'

He frowned. 'Is that such an awful idea?'

The resisted the urge to laugh hysterically. Was he trying to send her mad? 'I don't think that is a good idea.'

'The reason being?'

She shook her head, chuckling even though the conversation wasn't in the least funny. 'I've stopped making a fool of myself over you, Jake Harding.'

'It's only a cup of tea.' He looked exasperated. 'What's so foolish about that?'

She unlocked the car and threw her bag on the seat. 'You don't understand, do you?' She placed her hands on her hips. 'I can't be your friend, Jake, not after telling you that I loved you and being rejected.'

'Why?'

'Because it hurts too much.' Lord, he was dense!

He bowed his head, shuffling the polished toe of his shoe in the dirt. 'I am honoured that you think you love me.'

'I *know* I do.'

'You don't know me, Audrey,' he whispered.

'That isn't an excuse any more. We've lived in the same house for months. I know what it's like to feel your hand on me, to have you kiss me. You are kind and generous and care deeply for the people in your care. I've seen your many moods and I know you don't like tripe and your favourite meal is roast lamb. You've told me about your past and—.'

'Not all of it. I've done things I'm ashamed of. I'm not fit to be the person you can depend on.'

She took a step closer, her heart breaking with emotion. 'Shouldn't I be the judge of that? Besides, you're already dependable. The men and nurses at Twelve Pines depend on you.'

Jake crossed his arms, defensive. 'That's professional.'

'Meaning your heart isn't involved.'

'Correct.'

'I don't believe that for a moment.'

'It's true.'

She sighed and slid into the driver's side of the car. 'I feel so sorry for you.'

Her words struck home, and he straightened, his face tightening. 'I assure you there's no need to be sorry for me.' He walked around to the other side of the car and got in.

'What are you doing?'

'Bugger the tea. I feel like something much stronger. Can you drop me off at the nearest pub?'

'I'm sure getting drunk will solve all your problems,' she said tartly and started the engine.

'I never had a problem until I met you.'

She reversed out of the parking area and onto the road. 'Yes, you did, only you didn't face it.'

'You know nothing.'

'If that is what you want to believe, so be it. Isn't it strange that you can treat patients but not yourself? You hide away from it like a—'

'Stop the car.'

She braked and changed gear, pulling into the curb. 'Truth hurts?'

Emotions played across his face. His eyes narrowed. 'I'll not sit here and let you call me a coward again. I thought you were a nice person, but you're rude and opinionated. It's impossible to have a decent conversation with you.'

They sat in heated silence, staring out the window. Outside the world was going about its business. Women shopping with their ration cards, children playing in the street with hoops and spinning tops, a shopkeeper swept his shop step.

Audrey knew that whatever was said next would determine the future between them one way or another and there would be no going back. It was time to make or break.

'I never wanted to feel again, Audrey,' Jake whispered.

Her hands tightened on the steering wheel. 'I won't hurt you, Jake, not ever. Do you think I enjoy being so vulnerable? I never asked for this.'

'I know.' He nodded, placed his elbow against the passenger side window and banged the back of his knuckles against his chin. 'The whole situation has been arduous. I've had to make decisions, ones I never thought I would have to think about again.'

'Did you think that you could spend the rest of your life without feeling, without experiencing love? Did you want to live such a barren life?'

'Yes. The alternative was too difficult. Being dead inside isn't so bad.' He shrugged.

'It's no way to live.'

'I could have done it.'

'Until I came along and made you remember what it is like to be loved by another once more.'

He groaned. 'Yes, you made me remember and I wasn't ready to.'

'It can't have been easy for you to have me around, but I won't hide my feelings. I've fallen in love with you and there's not a lot I can do about it while you live under my roof.'

His blue eyes darkened to violet. 'I'm afraid of your feelings. More afraid of anything I've ever been before.'

Audrey put the car in gear and joined the small amount of traffic on the road. She headed to the promenade and found a park in front of a small hotel that overlooked the ocean. The afternoon was growing dark, clouds covered the sun, and a strong wind blew from the water. 'Come, let us walk.'

'It's too cold.'

She took a deep breath and let it out slowly. Out of her side window she saw the row of hotels that catered to the tourists in summer when there wasn't a war raging.

Jake shifted in his seat. 'I should tell you that this morning I used your telephone.'

'Oh?'

'I'm going away, to London, for a training course. I'll also be applying for a transfer.'

Inside she shrivelled up and died. He'd killed off any remaining hopes that they would be together.

'Also, I'm taking Nielson with me. I have organised for him to be seen by a friend who is a specialist doctor in the field of psychiatry. He has a home in Kent and works with cases like Nielson. I think he'll be able to help him more than I can because he's been studying that side of medicine for longer than I have.'

'I'm happy that Nielson will get more help.'

'I've also arranged that you'll get no more soldiers while I'm gone, and if you do, they'll not be serious cases, Doctor Penshaw will cope.'

Panic bubbled up inside. 'When do you go?'

'I've been given permission to leave tomorrow evening.'

'Will you come back? You'll not return after the training course to pack or anything?' she whispered, dreading the answer, but knowing it what it'll be.

'I'm not sure…No, I won't lie to you.' He let out a long breath. 'I have requested a transfer and it has been confirmed. I won't be coming back after I leave tomorrow.'

She moaned softly, burying the urge to beg him to stay. 'Am I that terrible?'

'No, Audrey-'

'I'm driving you away.' Her chest tightened that it had all come to this. She had been so stupid.

'No, you haven't, not entirely, but you have made me face certain things that I was keeping hidden away inside.' He took his cap off and ran his fingers through his hair. 'I can't deal with them while I'm near you. I need some time away.'

She covered her face with her hands. 'I'm sorry.'

'Don't be sorry. You've done nothing but fall in love, sadly it was with me.' He gave a mocking laugh. 'You poor sweetheart, your love is wasted on me.'

'Please forgive me. I've not made your time at Twelve Pines comfortable, always there, fawning over you.'

'You didn't fawn.'

'I am arrogant. I should have known that I couldn't make you love me. How silly of me, how conceited I am to think I could make you feel anything for me, especially after all you've been through.'

'Audrey, no, I-'

'Say you'll forgive me, Jake.' She raised her chin, finding some inner strength. 'I haven't handled this well. I have no experience dealing with falling in love. I don't know the rules.'

'Will you let me speak?' He grinned, taking her hands. 'You have nothing to be sorry about. All you've done is give, whereas I have behaved like a bloody fool.' The smile slipped away, and his eyes turned stormy. 'You don't know me, Audrey. I've done some things, terrible things that I'm ashamed of. That's partly why I'm leaving. I need to clear my head, as well as my heart of my past.'

'You must understand and not think I want to replace, Marianne, I don't. I never could. I just want to be with you.' Her bottom lip trembled with emotion, but she fought the tears. 'I happen to like your company.'

He brought her hands up to his lips and kissed them. 'I know, and I'm honoured, and somewhere in my confused mind, I know I want to be with you too.'

'You do?' She reared back shocked. 'But you sometimes behave as though you hate me. That the very sight of me repels you.'

'It's true. There were times when I hated you because you made me feel again, and I wasn't ready. I refused to think of you in any way but as a stranger, but you slowly broke down my defences.' He rubbed the back of his knuckles against her cheek. 'It was rather confronting, being openly chased by a beautiful woman, a good woman, who kept pushing past the rebuffs I gave her.'

'On occasion I wanted to give up, but each time I saw you or thought about you, I just loved you more. Even when you were acting ghastly towards me.'

'I'm sorry for that. I just need some time…'

Hope flared within her and she gripped his hands. 'I'll wait. No matter how long it takes, I'll wait for you to come back.'

'I'll not ask you to do that. I don't want to be responsible for your happiness, Audrey, I'm not ready for it.'

'You aren't responsible, I am, and I know that if I have to wait for you so eventually we can be together, then I will do it.'

His wry smile appeared. 'I don't even think I'm any good for you.'

'At least let us find out, yes?'

'Audrey…' He pulled her against him and held her tight.

She buried her face into his neck, breathing in the smell of him. Tears spilled. She held him tighter and closed her eyes as he responded the same way. If there was the slightest chance he could come to love her, then she was willing to take it. Her heart turned over as he whispered her name, and she kissed his neck above his collar. Over his shoulder she saw the row of guesthouses that faced the sea. She drew back and smiled at him. 'Will you spend the night with me in one of those?'

Jake twisted to look where she pointed. 'You want to-to—'

'Yes. I do,' she whispered. 'It may be all I ever have of you.'

'You must think this through properly, Audrey.'

She opened the car door and got out, waiting for him to do the same. They stared at each other over the top of the car for a long moment.

Jake slowly smiled. 'You sure? Really sure?'

Grinning, full of excitement, she nodded. 'Utterly.'

It seemed the simplest thing in the world to do. They walked into the first guesthouse and asked for a room. Without batting an eyelid, the owner asked them to sign the book, pay a deposit and then handed them their key.

Once in the room, very basic in furniture, but with a wonderful view looking over the ocean, Audrey looked at Jake and got the giggles. She felt like a naughty schoolgirl.

Jake thrust his hands in his trouser pockets and wrinkled his nose as he gazed about the room. 'Fancy getting some fish and chips?'

Her amusement left her at the sight of his straight face. Was he having second thoughts? Putting it off, hoping she'd change her mind? 'Oh um, yes.' She cleared her throat and forced herself to be cheerful. 'I'm starving.'

At the door he paused, and as she turned to him, he cupped one cheek and softly kissed her. 'We have all night, sweetheart.'

She melted against him, eager for whatever the night would bring. After another sweet tender kiss, they went downstairs holding hands. Audrey felt she was walking on air, as though she was high on a cloud watching the scene below. Could it be true that sensible Audrey Pearson was going to spend the night with the dashing army doctor, Captain Harding? Was it a dream?

Strolling the streets, her hand tucked warmly through his arm, they soon found a fish and chip shop. The aroma of vinegar wafting out the front door greeted them.

Audrey stayed beside Jake as he ordered their food. The large woman behind the counter laughed and chatted with him while she slapped their fish and chips into the newspaper and wrapped them up. It was the first time Audrey had seen Jake relaxed enough to laugh and joke. She liked it. Had she done this? Could it be possible that he was slowly returning to the happy man he once was before Marianne died? She shook her head and silently berated herself. *Don't rush things.*

One night.

She had but one night to really show him her love and give him something to take away with him. For a second she panicked, what is she was no good at *it*? She had no experience. Would she know what to do? But then he glanced over his shoulder and gave her a dazzling smile that made her sigh with devotion. It would be all right — it had to be.

They ate their fish and chips straight from the newspaper wrapper and strolled along the promenade, which at the start of the war had been closed off, but now, after 4 years, parts of it had gradually became free of clutter for people to amble. Above them, seagulls squawked, dipping and diving, hoping for a crumb to be thrown.

Audrey tilted her face to the sea, and the salt breeze. Contentment filled her. Here she was walking beside Jake in companionable silence, munching on vinegar-soaked chips and fresh fish cooked just right. For one night she didn't want to have a care in the world, wanted nothing to spoil what little time they had. Only, she knew he'd be thinking of other things. 'You are able to stay?'

He picked at his piece of fish. 'Doctor Penshaw is only a telephone call away and the nurses know how to use the telephone. I just pray the air raid siren doesn't sound. Nielson is getting better but he's not out of the woods yet. Something small could trigger him off.'

Guilt replaced the contentment. 'Would you prefer to go home?'

He stopped and gazed at her. 'No. Unless you've changed your mind?'

'Not at all.' She touched his cheek. 'I didn't want you worrying, that's all.'

'I'll ring the house and let them know then, shall I?' He winked.

'Yes, good idea.'

Jake stepped closer and rested his forehead against hers. 'I'm where I want to be. I can't predict the future, but right here and now, this is where I *need* to be.'

'Good.' She kissed him, tasting salt and vinegar. 'Let us go back.'

He nodded and taking her wrapper and his own, threw them in the nearest bin. 'First, I want to get a bottle of wine from somewhere. Let's celebrate this night in style. Yes?'

'Sounds wonderful, but I doubt we'll fine some.'

'A bottle of ale then?' He grinned.

'Not ale.' She shuddered. 'We might have to make do with a cup of tea.'

Laughing, they walked hand in hand down the street to the pub on the corner and Jake ran in to buy a bottle of whatever was available. He returned, triumphantly holding the wine bottle aloft. 'Don't let anyone say I can't celebrate in style.'

It was only when they had returned to the guesthouse and were alone in the room, did the gaiety leave her and she felt nervous. Jake opened the bottle of wine and found two small glasses on a wooden table by the window.

'Shall we toast?' he said, passing her a glass.

'Why not?' She raised the glass to join his.

'To tonight.'

'To tonight.' She smiled, while silently adding, *and to the future whatever it brings.*

Jake took a sip, watching her. 'What are you thinking about?'

She shrugged and stepped away to go look out the window. 'Being here with you. Wondering if it's only a dream.'

He came to stand behind her. 'Maybe it is a dream, maybe we should wake up.'

'Why would you want to?'

'Because I don't want you being hurt, Audrey. This is all so uncertain. My feelings are uncertain.'

She spied a boat on the water in the distance. 'Well, mine aren't even if yours are.'

'You're not frightened?'

'A little.' She stepped closer, wanting him to hold her and was grateful when he took their wine, placed it on the table and then folded her into a tight embrace. They stayed that way as the sky darkened into grey twilight.

Finally, Jake took her hand and guided her over to the bed and they sat on the edge. 'I want to talk to you and tell you some things before we commit to spending the night together.'

She nodded and waited. The room grew dim with they only light being the twilight coming in the window. She had no urge to draw the blackouts and switch on the lamp. Shadows played across Jake's face.

'When…' He took a deep breath. 'When Marianne and the baby died, I was grief stricken and very angry. Full of rage. I took it as a personal slight against me. I couldn't understand their deaths and why it had to happen to me. I wasn't a bad person so why me?'

He stood and walked to the window. 'I spent the first week after their deaths dead drunk. My mother tried to help me, but I abused her good nature. I was such a bastard to her. I told her to leave me to rot and, in the end, she did. She walked out of my flat and went home. Now, of course, I am filled with shame, but back then I didn't care. Nothing affected while I was in that state.'

Audrey sent him a look of concern. 'I'm sure she would understand.'

'Yes, she does now, but that doesn't make it right.'

'You were grieving.'

'That's not the worst of it. I wish it was.' Jake turned away and stared out the window. 'When I rejoined my unit, I behaved unprofessionally. I was drinking heavily to forget Marianne. The problem was I hadn't worn off the effects of the drinking by morning and still continued to work as a doctor. I made bad judgements.' He shuddered. 'Looking back, it was lucky I didn't kill someone, though it came close to it once or twice. Instead, I made stupid mistakes that other colleagues noticed. My moods, the rude way I spoke to people and patients became unacceptable, but I didn't care. In the end I was transferred to France. They, the hospital, the army, whoever, wanted rid of me. Who could blame them?'

'What happened then?' she whispered.

'Something in me snapped. I stopped drinking, but no longer cared whether I lived or died. The hospital I was stationed at wasn't close enough to the front line for my liking. I requested a transfer and got it. Next thing I knew I was in a field hospital near Dunkirk.'

'Dunkirk?' She remembered the devastation that swept the country when Dunkirk was surrounded by the German forces. Then, the jubilation when so many were rescued.

'Yes. I was there, well, not in the town. We were stationed outside a small village in that area. Strangely I thrived on the chaos, the bloodshed, the fear. Their suffering fed my suffering. I wasn't alone in it, and-and at that time, I think I wanted other people to hurt too, as I was doing.'

'Come sit beside me.' Audrey patted the bed. He did what she asked, wiping a hand across his forehead. She wanted to erase the tortured expression from his face.

As soon as he sat, he was up again, pacing the floor in the muted light. 'I felt…liberated in a way. It's hard to explain.' He shifted his weight from foot to foot.

'I think you're doing a good job of explaining. Tell me more.'

He stopped and stared out of the window once more, his back to her. 'The field hospital was over run, or very nearly. A German advance caught up with the last of us who had to wait for more ambulances to come pick us up…' He was silent for a moment. 'I had three patients, soldiers who weren't as badly wounded as the others, that's why they were in the last batch to go. I offered to stay with them and let the others evacuate.'

Audrey remained very still, allowing him to tell the story his own way without interruption.

'The German advance reached us quickly, and we knew they'd search in the buildings first, so we ran and hid along a bank near the road. The enemy searched what remained of the hospital, which was only a large barn really. Anyway, we heard the shouts, orders given and so we scuttled further along the bank, hoping to God we wouldn't be found. I didn't care if I died, but I wasn't going to get my patients killed if I could help it.'

He leaned his forearm up against the pane. 'Two scouts were sent to explore the area. I knew we were in trouble as soon as they came our way. We didn't have any cover and once they stood on the bank, they'd see us. So, I told the soldiers to shuffle down, cross through the water and hide in a small woodland area on the other side. The only problem was we were further away from the road and the chance of being rescued now became pretty slim.'

Jake wiped a hand over his face. 'I kept watch while the others crept towards the woodland. Next thing I knew a gun was pointed at my head from above. A German solider stood on the bank. Oddly though he'd not called out to attract attention. I'll never forget his face, a mask really, devoid of all emotion. He climbed down the bank and came up very close to me. I had my arms up in surrender and he searched me for weapons. I had none of course, being a doctor.'

Audrey gazed at his strong profile, her heart breaking at the tremor in his voice. She ached to hold him, to offer any comfort, but she knew she couldn't, not yet.

'To this day I still don't understand how it happened. I guess it was because we stood on a sloping bank, but the German stumbled, and my reflexes were quicker than his. When he lost his balance, I snatched at his rifle. We wrestled, fell to the ground and rolled into the stream. I hated getting my boots wet because wet socks cause so many foot problems. It's bizarre what goes through your mind at the most unlikely times.' He shrugged. 'It was the last straw though in my wretched life. I completely lost my temper. I grabbed the rifle and smashed the butt into his face...I couldn't stop. I just kept hitting him over and over.'

A shiver ran through Audrey's body, her hands clutched the bedcovers.

'That was the very worst moment of my life, Audrey, the very worst.'

She swallowed. 'You did what you had to. It's survival.'

'No, you don't understand.'

'Then explain it to me.'

Jake shook his head and finally turned to face her. The darkness of the room hid his features but the slumped set of his shoulders and low tone of his voice told her the pain he suffered. 'I'm a doctor! I swore an oath to save lives, not take them. Can't you see what I've done?'

'But it's war, Jake. Everything changes in a war. It's madness.'

'That's no excuse, not to me it isn't. I killed a man!'

'Yes, to save your life and that of three others.'

'I'm not a solider. I'm a doctor that is the difference. I had no right to do what I did.'

'Nonsense!' She jerked to her feet. 'How dare you be such a martyr!'

He stiffened. 'Pardon?'

'You heard,' she snapped. 'I won't have you condemning yourself because you killed one person when out there,' she threw out her arm towards the window, 'across that sea, thousands of men are dying and killing every day. What makes you so special?'

Astonishment etched his face. 'Because my job is to heal not kill.'

'And you think theirs is? Do you think that they all want to kill another man?' She sucked in a gasp of air.

'They are trained soldiers!'

'Because its war. If it weren't, would they be killers? No. Before the world went mad, they were butchers, farmers, shopkeepers, clerks, the list is endless. My brother was the sweetest, most gentle person I knew. Do you think he wanted to kill another man? Do you think it was easy for him? Is it easy for any of them? You aren't so unique, Jake.'

'I guess not.' He spoke very quietly, his head lowered. 'But it doesn't stop the shame I feel and the guilt which eats away at me.'

She ran to him, holding him tight and pressing his head into her neck. 'I'm sorry, darling, for being so hateful, I really am, but you have to stop tormenting yourself. Does anyone behave normally in the midst of war?'

He stood stiff and unresponsive for a second and then sagged against her, crushing her to him. After a moment, he raised his head. 'Are we behaving normally?'

She smiled and pulled his head down to kiss him. 'Who cares for normality?'

He kissed her again and then went to switch on the lamp. The soft light filled the room, pushing the darkness into the corners. 'Now you know my darkest secrets, what do you think of me?'

She sat on the bed and studied him as he drank down a gulp of wine. 'Did you tell me in hope of pushing me away?'

The corners of his sensual mouth lifted in a wry smile. 'Perhaps. There may have been a part of me that wanted you to run away.'

'Why?' She gave him a severe look. 'So, you can go on living a lonely existence?'

'At least my life was simple.'

'It was no life at all, and you know it.'

He nodded. Tiredness lined his face.

Audrey kicked off her shoes and crawled up the bed. After plumping up the pillows, she lay down. 'Come here.'

'Audrey…'

'Jake, take off your shoes and lie down beside me. You're tired and need some sleep.'

His eyes widened. 'Sleep?'

She grinned. 'Yes, sleep.'

The bed shifted one side when he sat on it to take off his shoes. Her stomach clenched as he moved further onto the bed and stretched out. Side by side, they turned their heads and stared at each other. Gently, with the lightest touch, Audrey traced his jaw line with her fingertip. The contact was enough for him to groan and pull her close against him. She glorified in his embrace, the way one of his hands spanned her stomach. 'Go to sleep, my love.'

'I can't.' He kissed her temple.

She shifted position so that she could lay his head on her chest, her arms wrapped around him. 'Sleep darling.'

'But I thought you want to—'

'The time will come for that, but for now you need to sleep. You're exhausted.' She kissed the top of his head and stroked his back in long slow movements. Her body ached for his touch, but he needed to unwind.

'I won't sleep. I never do.'

'Then we'll lie here quiet together and forget the rest of the world.'

He heaved a long sigh. 'I like the sound of that.'

Soon she felt him relax against her, then minutes later his breathing slowed and became regular. She kissed him again and smiled. This wasn't the night as she planned when first asking him, but what did it matter? They had shared something else that was just as special. Who'd have thought that tonight Jake would open himself to her? He didn't have to. She actually doubted he ever would. He could have simply had sex with her and kept his mind closed. But he had opened up, and she loved him all the more for it, because he trusted her with his darkest secrets and thoughts.

She tightened her embrace, and he didn't stir. His slept deeply, a healthy sleep he needed. Closing her eyes, she relaxed. She didn't know what the future would bring, but she knew she didn't want the morning to come.

Chapter Twelve

Audrey stooped, cut the cabbage stem and lifted the vegetable clean from soil. She gazed down at the nearly depleted row. The September days were cooling, bringing to an end another summer. The weather wasn't all that had changed.

The previous week, the nation had quietly acknowledged the fifth anniversary of the outset of war. Five years. Such a long time. They called it a National Day of Prayer, but Audrey hadn't prayed. Her faith had been lost the day Robbie died, her prayers for his wellbeing hadn't helped him then. What did she have to pray for now? The war would end when it ended, and nothing she did could alter that. She was more worried about what would happen once the war had finished. What would be left? A worn-out country with so many men vanished, struggling widows, and fatherless children.

She kicked at a clump of dirt and looked back at the house. Everything looked old, worn out and tired. The trees were changing colour, the greenness bleaching out of the landscape each day, to be replaced by the dull grey of winter.

A quietness had settled on Twelve Pines. The men and nurses had gone with no word of when any more would be sent to replace them. Jake had said he'd try to make sure they'd receive no more patients, but she hadn't been prepared for the silence to descend like a heavy cloak. She and Lucy crept around the house that no longer felt like a home. Two people living in a house that size was ridiculous.

Audrey sighed and fiddled with the cabbage, checking it for bugs. Most days she was alone in the house, as Lucy found any excuse to be away with friends. Without Lucy's company she missed Jake even more. He left over three weeks ago and had sent only one letter. She touched her overall's pocket. The letter crinkled within. It was in no way a love letter, which at first saddened her, instead Jake wrote of practical matters, travelling to Kent, settling in Neilson, attending lectures, visiting hospitals for re-turned soldiers. So many things kept him occupied, while she sat alone in a large house and pretended she was doing her bit too. Sadly, she knew this wasn't the case, not anymore. But what to do about it? Join up? Then what would she do about Lucy?

Some part of her told her to just wait. Wait for the war to end, wait for Jake to come back to her, wait for Lucy to marry and leave home. Only she was tired of watching life go by without actually feeling as though she was involved.

'Miss Pearson.'

Audrey jumped, startled out of her thinking by Owen's call from the top of the vegetable garden. 'Yes?'

'There's a telephone call for you.'

'Oh, thank you.' She left the garden, hurried around the glasshouses and ran across the yard through into the kitchen, where she dumped the cabbage on the sideboard.

Mrs Graham stood at the table chopping carrots. She looked up with a smile. 'There you are. A call for you from Captain Harding.'

Audrey's stomach fluttered as she raced through the hall to the black telephone mounted on the wall by the front door. Picking up the receiver, she paused to get her breath. 'Jake?'

'Audrey? Yes, it's me. Where were you? I've been waiting ages.'

'I was down the back garden cutting cabbages.'

'Typical. Always got your hands dirty.' His soft laughter warmed her heart. 'Listen, I don't have much time, but I wanted to hear your voice. I've been thinking about you. I'll be getting leave soon—'

'Wonderful!'

'No, it isn't, it's only a day pass and not enough time for me to come up and see you. I'm to report to a London hospital. I'll be working there for the foreseeable future. I'll send you the details in a letter.'

'Oh, I see.' She hoped he didn't hear her disappointment. 'Did you get my letters?'

'Yes. Damn.' She heard him mumbled to someone else before he came back to her. 'I have to go. There are people wanting the telephone.'

'Yes, of course.'

'I'll call again in a day or two. My friend in Kent didn't have the telephone at his house. There nearest one was ten miles away.'

'Where are you now?'

'I'm on my way to see my mother and then returning to London.' Noise in the background interrupted him again. 'Audrey? Audrey, I have to go.'

'Yes… Well, thank you for calling.'

'Is everything all right with you?'

'Absolutely.' She smiled into the mouthpiece. 'Nothing ever happens here, you know that.'

'Look after yourself...' More noise crackled in her ear. 'Goodbye, Audrey...'

'Goodbye, Jake, goodbye.' The telephone line went dead, and she stood leaning against the wall completely shattered by the enormity of how much she missed him.

The front door opened, and Lucy came in.

Audrey straightened and replaced the telephone on its cradle. 'You're home.'

'Obviously,' Lucy snapped, striding by into the drawing room.

'Is something wrong?' Audrey followed her and became alarmed when Lucy took the brandy bottle from the cabinet and poured a large measure into a glass.

'There is always something wrong, sister dear.' Lucy waved the glass at her. 'Don't you know there's a war on?'

Audrey stiffened at her tone and the brittle look in Lucy's eyes. 'You seem upset.'

'No…I'm just having a drink.'

'In the middle of the day?'

'Does it matter?'

'Yes, it matters.' Peering hard at Lucy, Audrey detected that this wasn't the first drink of the day. Lucy's eyes were bloodshot, and she swayed slightly. Shivers of fear tingled up her spine. 'What's happened?'

'Would you care?' Lucy asked loftily. She strolled over to the window and stared out.

Frightened not only by her behaviour but also by her words, Audrey stepped closer. 'You know I care. What is this nonsense?'

'Nonsense, is it?' Lucy laughed without humour. 'What do you know of my life recently, sister dear? You're so wrapped up in your own little world, a world that doesn't exceed the boundaries of Twelve Pines.'

Audrey swallowed, shocked at the distance that had grown between them. It was true. In the last few months, she's not been deeply interested in Lucy's comings and goings. But then, she'd only been with friends doing her normal things, hadn't she, like attending dance halls, watching movies.

Lucy chuckled in a mocking way. 'You have no idea what I've been doing, have you?'

'Stop this. You're frightening me.' Audrey walked to the door. 'I'll not listen to you when you're acting this way.'

'You never listen to me.'

At the door, Audrey turned back. 'That's not true and you know it.'

Lucy shrugged, drank the last of the brandy and went to refill her glass.

'Don't have any more. I think you've had enough.'

'I'll have what I like.' Lucy filled the glass to the brim and then drank from the bottle.

'Lucy!' Audrey jerked forward and snatched the bottle from her. 'Stop this! What wrong with you. You're acting so—'

'So what? Strangely? Irrationally?' Lucy laughed so hard she choked. Audrey went to comfort her, but Lucy stumbled away, holding her hands in front to warn her off. 'Go away, Audrey. You can't help me now.'

'What are you talking about?' Audrey grabbed Lucy's hand. 'Tell me, please.'

Shaking her head, Lucy sat down with a plop on the window seat. 'You can't help me. Oh, God!' She buried her head in her hands. 'It's all such a mess. Such a *mess*!'

'Lord, Lucy, you're scaring me,' Audrey said in a low voice.

Sobs racked Lucy and Audrey hurried to enfold her in a tight embrace. 'I have you now. Shhh…' She rocked her sister as though she was a baby, cradling her head on her shoulder. The violence of Lucy's crying wounded her, and she was determined to get to the bottom of it. 'Have you been hurt? Did someone threaten you?'

Lucy hiccupped and leaned back. Her makeup smudged, hair in disarray, she reminded Audrey of when they were little and played dress ups in their mother's clothes. 'Don't hate me, please,' she whispered.

'I won't hate you, not ever.' Had her silly sister played a prank that had gone wrong? She fished in her pocket and brought out a crumpled handkerchief and gave it to her.

'I'm…I'm having a-a baby.' Lucy broke out into fresh weeping, burying her face in her hands.

Audrey jerked back as though slapped. She blinked, her mind not absorbing the words. No. It couldn't be right what Lucy just said.

Lucy looked up, her eyes red and swollen. 'Say something!'

'Are-are you sure?' Yes, it could be a ghastly mistake.

'Fairly sure. I've not had my period for two months.'

Audrey stood and paced the floor, nibbling her fingernails. 'Right. Two months.' Then she stopped abruptly, as the realisation that her little sister had sex. 'Who? I mean, why? You're only eighteen! Why did you do this and who with? Was it Robert? The messenger fellow? I knew he liked you, but—'

'Robert?' Lucy laughed without humour. 'As if he'd be the one, really.'

'Then who?'

'Ralph.'

Ralph? Audrey rubbed her forehead, trying to place the name with a face. 'Who is this Ralph person?'

Lucy stared at her. 'The man you aimed a gun at!'

Her mouth dropped open. That slimy smarmy fellow? The one who thought he had the charm to go with his good looks. 'No. Say it isn't true, you've got it wrong. Not him.'

'There is nothing wrong with Ralph.' Lucy sat straighter; her manner defensive. 'You have seen him only once and that wasn't a great night. You don't know him.'

'Well, *you* obviously do!' she snapped. 'I can't believe you've done this with him of all people.'

'Don't make judgements, Audrey, you know nothing about him. He's nice. He thinks the world of me.'

'Nice?' Audrey barked. 'What of love? Does he care for you enough to marry you?'

Lucy paled and her bottom lip trembled. 'I don't know.'

'So, you've not told him that you might be with child?'

'Might be? I think I have a reason enough to believe it's true.'

'Until we see a doctor, we'll think positive. You could be just late.'

'Two months late?' Lucy didn't look convinced. 'I doubt it.'

Audrey sat down on a chair near Valerie's old desk. They had put this room back to its original state yet, and she had a crazy idea to do it now. Anything was better than facing the fact her eighteen-year-old sister was having a child out of wedlock. Of all the foolish things to do! For the first time she was glad her parents were dead. This news would have devastated them.

'What are we going to do, Aud?' Lucy whispered.

Taking a deep breath, Audrey felt her anger leave when Lucy said, *we*. Her silly sister needed her, and despite her recent behaviour, she was still such an innocent. 'First, we'll ask Doctor Penshaw to examine you and see if it's true.'

Lucy groaned. 'Old Penshaw is a gossip.'

'We have no one else. He's been the family doctor since I was born.'

'Can we go to Scarborough? Or Hull? There's bound to be doctors there. Someone who doesn't know us.'

Tapping her fingernails on the desk, Audrey thought it over. It did make sense. 'Hull would be better. Father had business friends on Scarborough, and I'd hate to run into them outside a doctor's office.'

'Yes. Yes, we'll go to Hull,' Lucy said eagerly. 'Can we go this afternoon? There could be a train.'

'Not this afternoon. I'll have to find a doctor there and make an appointment.'

'Of course.' Lucy twisted the handkerchief in her hands.

'Why don't you go up and have a bath.' Audrey stood and went to the door. 'I'll make some calls. Mrs Graham has a sister in Hull. She may know of a doctor to telephone.'

'Excellent idea. A bath will be lovely.' Lucy followed her out but paused at the bottom of the stairs. 'Everything will be all right, won't it?'

Audrey patted her hand. 'Let us visit the doctor and see what happens there. We must take it one step at a time and deal with as it happens. We may be worrying over nothing.'

'Lord, I hope so. I never thought this would happen to me.'

'It wouldn't have done if you'd been sensible.'

'Don't, Audrey.' Lucy winced. 'You can't think worse of me than I do myself. I made a mistake, that's all.'

'The worst part is you lied to me. I never thought you'd lie to me.' Tears welled but she refused to give into the misery. 'All those times I believed you were at the cinema or with a friend, and instead you were with him.'

'It wasn't like that, not all the time. I did go to the cinema and out with friends. Only most of those times Ralph came along too.' Lucy rubbed her fingers. 'I couldn't resist his charm. Out of all the girls he sought me out. *Me.* And I felt special. I never meant to lie.' She turned and carried on up the stairs.

Audrey watched her go upstairs and then looked at the telephone. They had been the first in the area to install the machine and for days they had a stream of visitors coming to inspect it. At the time her Father thought it a great expense, but Robbie had been cocka-hoop about it. She had been sceptical about it, wondering if it would ever be used.

Thinking about her former reservations, she smiled. The instrument had become such an important part of their lives. Before it's been used to summon the doctor or call friends with good news. However, recently, it'd become a way for Jake to ring her and make him close even though he was miles away. The telephone would also be a way for her to contact a strange doctor and make an appointment for Lucy. Who would have thought it?

~ ~ ~

Audrey and Lucy stepped down the stone stairs leading to the docks. The grey afternoon sky and blustery conditions didn't help their mood. Behind them the city of Hull lay damaged and broken from constant air raids to destroy the dock and ships in the harbour. Seagulls cried, buffeted by the wind. Dockmen worked like bees in a hive, scurrying here and there, whistles blew, cranes swung cargo and

Why they picked such a crowded and noisy area, Audrey didn't know, but they had simply walked from leaving the doctor's office and kept going, each locked in their own private thoughts. The news that Lucy was pregnant had dashed Audrey's slim hopes that all this would be over with today. Instead, they had so much more to sort out than they imagined.

'I miss Valerie,' Lucy murmured, head down against the gale.

'I do too.' Audrey pulled her coat collar up higher. Valerie would have been strong in this predicament. Would have known what to do and how to act. After all, she'd been through it herself. However, Val was miles away in France, serving her country, soothing wounded men far from home.

'Could we get a cup of tea? I'm cold.'

Nodding, Audrey slipped her hand through Lucy's arm and the walked on to the next set of stairs leading back up to street level. Across the road they spotted a small tearoom and hurried inside.

They chose a table by the taped-up window and ordered a pot of tea and cheese sandwiches while they took off their gloves. The tearoom held only a few customers and had nothing of interest to look at.

Lucy sighed and played with the sugar bowl. 'I might miscarry, you know.' Her voice dropped to a whisper. 'Or I could get rid of it. Girls do it all the time. Apparently, there's a woman in Beverly who does it for a few quid. A friend told me so. That would solve it all.'

'Don't talk rubbish!' Audrey shuddered and leant across the table to whisper back. 'You'll not be going to any back-alley abortionist. Really, Lucy, I do wonder at the friends you keep. Miscarriages and *getting rid of it* can cause the woman to bleed too much. If you haemorrhage badly enough, you can die.'

'The alternative is to have it then.'

They sat back as the waitress, an elderly lady, brought them their order on a tray. When she'd returned to the counter, Audrey swirled the teapot around while Lucy added sugar to their cups and a drop of milk.

'The next thing is to decide what to do now.' She poured out the tea and placed the teapot on the tray.

'I have the baby, obviously. There is nothing to decide.'

'Oh, do grow up, Lucy, for heaven's sake.' Audrey glared at the sullen expression her sister wore. 'You do have choices. You either marry Dolton or have the baby adopted.'

'You make it sound so easy.' Lucy pushed her sandwiches away and stared out the window.

Audrey swallowed her frustration. 'Tell me about Dolton. Will he marry you? Is he from a good family?'

'I have no idea.' Lucy shrugged.

'You don't sound as if you know him at all.'

'We never talked much. There were always others with us.'

'Not all the time, obviously.'

Lucy sent her a sarcastic grimace. 'Very funny.'

'Actually, there isn't anything remotely funny about it. You'll have to tell him when we get home.'

'I suppose so.'

Audrey sipped her tea and summoned up her patience. 'How will he take it?'

Lucy reared back. 'How should I know? He's a man, isn't he? He's likely to go crazy and we'll never see him again.'

'He sounds like a charmer, Lucy.' She bit into her sandwich. 'Do you want to marry him?'

'It's hardly just my choice, is it? He has to want to as well.'

'Forget him for a moment. I'm asking you. Do *you* want him?'

'I could do worse I suppose.'

'This isn't a joke, you know. This is very serious. Marriage is for life. Could you spend your life with him?'

'I don't know. Maybe.'

'Oh, help me out here, Lucy. I'm trying my best.'

Lucy pushed the bowl away. 'What do you want me to say? I don't have the answers, Audrey, I really don't.'

'No, you want me to fix it for you. Well, I can't, Lucy. Not by myself.'

'There is nothing to fix because it can't be fixed. My life is over, ruined. One stupid mistake has led to this!'

'Keep your voice down,' Audrey ground out. 'You only have yourself to blame. You and Dolton are responsible for this mess. So, don't take it out on me. You want to act the grown up so start now.'

'Oh, leave me alone, Audrey.' Lucy leaned forward across the table. 'You think yourself so perfect, but I saw how you were with Captain Harding. Panting after him like a bitch on heat. No wonder the poor man ran from you. Couldn't get away quick enough.'

Before Audrey could respond to Lucy's shocking words, the air raid siren sounded. A collective groan came from the other customers and the waitress began turning off the kitchen equipment.

'Come on, we'll have to follow the others and find the nearest shelter.' Audrey stood and gathered her purse and gloves. Lucy's heated accusation not only shocked her, but they hurt too. Did everyone think of her as Lucy did?

'No, I'm not coming.' Lucy sipped her tea as though everything was all right.

'Don't be silly. This isn't like home. The Germans actually intend for their bombs to drop on Hull not just pass over like they do near us.'

'I don't care. A bomb would suit me just fine, actually.'

'Stop your dramatics.' Audrey grabbed her arm, spilling the tea. 'Get your things.'

The waitress hurried over. 'You must get to a shelter quickly.'

'Where is the nearest one?' Audrey asked, pulling Lucy up from her seat.

'Up the road, there's a cellar that we use.' The waitress held the door open while everyone left.

'You don't have one?' Audrey asked.

'Ours has a foot of water in it. The bombs have shaken the foundations and water's seeping in from the docks.'

The drone of the planes cut off the chance for further conversation and they all ran up the road, following the waitress, who despite her age could move quickly.

At the entrance to the alley leading to the cellar, Lucy balked and ripped her hand out of Audrey's. 'I'm not going in.'

'Come on, Lucy.' Audrey went to grab her again, but Lucy spun out of reached and raced back down the street.

'Lucy!' Audrey screamed. Without thought, she chased after her. The planes were getting closer. The air seemed to vibrate with the noise of plane engines and the wailing air raid siren. She would slap her brainless sister stupid once she got hold of her.

Ahead, Lucy rounded and corner. Audrey jumped to the gutter to follow, but the heel of her shoe caught in a drain grill and her foot twisted. She went down with a thump on her knees, scraping her hands. Her gloves and purse went flying away to land by a shop wall.

A little stunned, Audrey sat on her bottom and bit her lip in pain as she touched her sore ankle. Her hands throbbed and blood pebbled on the scratches.

'Are you all right, Miss?' A young boy was beside her before she realised.

'I've hurt my ankle. Can you help me up, please?'

'Yes, Miss.' Freckles covered his face, and he was as skinny as a stick, but together they managed to get her up on one foot. 'You can lean on me, Miss.'

'No, help me to the wall there, and then get to a shelter. I'll be simply fine.'

His blue eyes widened. 'Eh, Miss, I can't leave you.'

'Yes, you can and will.' She hopped, with his help, to the protection of the shop wall and leant against it. 'Now, go. I'll wait here a minute. My sister will be back shortly.'

'But the bombs.' He jumped beside her as the first bombs whistled through the air. 'We have to get to a shelter.'

The loud boom of a bomb landing on a building erupted behind them, only streets away.

Audrey looked up at the planes and watched in fascination as the bombs dropped to the earth with shattering regularity. She pushed the boy away. 'You go, now, hurry. I mean it.' She pushed him again, and he darted off without a backward glance.

Around her the world went mad. The crashing, roaring explosions as the bombs destroyed the city filled her ears. The wall she rested against shook with every blast. Plumes of grey dust floated down the street. She heard screaming, the siren of a fire engine and above it all the continued whistles of flying bombs.

She had to find some cover. A bomb landed a few streets away and Audrey ducked down low, the blast rumbling the ground beneath her. She looked up as more planes flew directly overhead. Their undercarriages opened and spilled out their weapons of destruction.

Frozen in horror, Audrey watched the missiles descend and knew she wouldn't come out of this alive. Her last thought as the surrounding buildings blew up was of Jake, and the way he smiled.

Chapter Thirteen

Shouting woke her. So much noise. Her head pounded and shapes were muted and blurry, out of focus. Audrey blinked, but found there was grit in her eyes. She wiped them with her sleeve and the smell of dust and cement went up her nose, and she jerked away. Her eyes watering from the dust particles and grit, she tried to make out her surroundings. She was dimly aware of shouting above her, but her immediate environment was nothing more than a few square feet of space walled in by debris of brick and wood. Everything was grey, the light, the air, her clothes and her crumbling prison.

Then it hit her. She'd been bombed. But she had survived. Relief washed over her. She had to get out. Above her was a gap in the collapsed building. If she could just climb up there a bit…

Her head ached like the worst headache she'd ever had, but her ankle throbbed more where it was twisted up under her. Shifting her weight, Audrey tried to ease the pressure on her ankle. A piece of wood near her shoulder moved, sending more dust into the air. Coughing, she kept as still as possible, scared the rubble would topple in on top of her.

'Help! Help. I'm in here.' Her voice came out croaky and insignificant. The hammering and noise continued, and she doubted she could be heard.

She thought fleetingly of Lucy. Was she safe? Did Lucy know what had happened to her? Would they keep digging? Did they even know she was in here? Her head hurt when she tried to think, and she was very thirsty. Her throat felt raw and dry. A nice cup of tea would be wonderful…

When she next woke it took her a moment to realise where she was. Darkness filled her little cave, and it was eerily quiet. Where was the noise? Had they all gone? Shaking from cold, she sat up and listened again. Nothing. They'd forgotten about her!

Panic bubbled up inside. 'Help! Help,' she screamed. 'Can anyone hear me?'

'Help.' She scrambled up onto her knees, banging her head on a piece of timber in the process. 'Help! I'm down here.'

She paused and listened. Nothing.

Whimpering with fright, Audrey looked above, hoping to see some light. 'Is anyone there?'

Please, please let there be someone.

Bowing her head, she sought for courage as tears gathered hot behind her lashes. She was going to die in this black hole. She moaned, terrified, then screamed and kept on screaming until her voice gave out and, when a blackness clouded her mind, she gladly gave into it.

~ ~ ~

Jake hurried through Hull's hospital entrance and towards the reception desk. Crowds of people stood or sat in the foyer, all with the same expression he imaged was on his face. The woman behind the counter was talking to a nurse and he was just about to interrupt them and ask for information on Audrey, when he heard his name.

'Captain Harding!' Lucy rushed to him and gripped his arms. She looked dreadful. 'How did you know? Did you telephone home?'

'Yes, Mrs Graham told me the news. How is she?'

'It was awful.'

He wanted to shake Lucy as she sobbed into her hands, her words mumbled and incoherent. 'Lucy! Is she alive?'

She raised her head and looked startled. 'Yes. Yes, she still lives.'

'Thank God.' He bent to catch his breath, feeling quite winded.

'Did you think she had died?'

'I didn't know what to think or expect. It's been agony.'

'She's still unconscious.'

'Her other injuries?'

Frowning, Lucy dabbed at her eyes with a handkerchief. 'None that I know of, but the staff hardly tell me anything.'

'I must see her.'

'Come this way. I can take you to her. It's family only, but I'll say you're a cousin or something.'

He nodded and took her arm to speed her along the wide corridors. For the last two days his heart seemed lodged in his throat. Two days! He couldn't believe his bad luck since hearing the news about Audrey from Mrs Graham. Everything that could go wrong went wrong. He couldn't get leave immediately and had to finish his shift at the hospital, then he missed his train. Finally, he managed to take another, only to find he had to make three connections, with the last train breaking down for over six hours.

'It's good of you to come,' Lucy said, slowing down and turning left.

'Naturally, I'd come.' He thanked the fates that made him ring Twelve Pines. Yet, when Mrs Graham told him of the catastrophe that happened in Hull, he thought his heart would give out altogether. It wasn't until that moment that he truly acknowledged his love for Audrey.

Before a white painted door, Lucy hesitated. 'She's in here by herself because she hasn't woken up yet.' She led him into a stark white room, a room he'd seen a hundred times.

Audrey lay on an iron framed bed, the pallor of her face blending in with the white sheets and blanket. Her black curls, dust still clinging to them, stood out as any colour. A large bump had risen on her temple and would soon be an ugly bruise.

Jake stood beside her and tucked her hand into his. She was warm to touch, not hot, so no fever. He mentally inspected her as a doctor and then read her chart hanging at the end of the bed.

'She won't die will she, Captain?' Lucy murmured.

'I don't have the answers.'

'But she is all I have left. There must be something the doctors can do?'

'We won't know more until she regains consciousness.' He took her hand again and sat on the wooden chair beside the bed. 'She's had a blow to the head and then was left exposed to the elements, but the main thing is she has no other injuries that they can find. No broken bones.'

'She will wake up though?'

'Only Audrey can decide that.' He gazed at her pale face and the scratch on her temple. 'It's remarkable that she survived at all.'

'Yes…' Lucy cried into a handkerchief. 'I'll never forget the moment I went back to the street.'

'Why weren't you together?'

'I-we'd quarrelled. I was angry with her and upset. I ran off just as the planes came. I thought she'd gone down to the shelter.'

His lips tightened in anger. 'You know she'd never have a thought to her own safety while you were out during an air raid.'

'I thought she would because we'd argued. I thought she'd teach me a lesson and not come after me.' She gave a little hiccup. 'I was terrified. So many bombs, more than I could count. When the all clear sounded, I went back to the street near the docks. There was nothing left of the street only rubble, broken buildings…'

His stomach churned. So close. He'd been so close to losing her.

Lucy straightened her shoulders and lifted her chin. 'I searched and called out her name for hours. The fire brigade came and helped. The cellar we were meant to go down took a direct hit. If I hadn't run, then we'd both be dead.' She shivered.

'Fate has amazing ways of changing our lives.'

'When I got back to the street and saw it all destroyed, I thought I'd died. I can't lose her too, Captain. I can't. She's the only family I have now.'

'Yes, I know she is.' His anger left as quickly as it came. 'What happened next?'

'It got dark and they lost hope of finding her alive because the others in the cellar were carried out dead.

But I didn't give up. Audrey hadn't been found in the cellar and I wasn't leaving until we found her. I begged them to look from one end to the other. They finally located her as dawn was breaking.'

'Was she awake?'

'No. I thought she was dead, but they said she wasn't.'

'You look exhausted, Lucy.' He took in her dishevelled appearance. The dirt mark on her skirt, her curls in disarray. 'Have you slept?'

'No, not really.' She twisted her handkerchief, her eyes swollen. 'I've stayed beside Audrey. They let me sleep on the chair.'

'You go book into a hotel and have a bath and some sleep. I'll stay with Audrey.'

'No, I couldn't.' She looked frightened and so very young. 'I couldn't leave her.'

'Do you have any money with you?'

'No, but I could go to the bank and take some from my account.'

'Yes, good idea. Buy some clothes too. Do you have some coupons?'

She shook her head, her chin wobbling with fresh tears. 'I don't have them with me. We were only coming here to see the doctor, not shopping.'

'Doctor?' Jake stared at her. 'Why?'

Lucy blushed and looked away. 'For me. Not Audrey.'

He took his cap off and ran his fingers through his hair. 'It might be best for you to go home and change. Come back in the morning.'

She stared at him. 'I won't leave her.'

'Lucy, when she wakes up and sees you in that state she'll worry and think you've not been looking after yourself. We don't want that, do we?'

Doubt showed in her eyes. 'No, I suppose not.'

'Go home and rest. Then you'll be refreshed for her when she needs you.'

'When they brought her out, I promised her I wouldn't leave her. I know she couldn't hear me, but I still promised.' Lucy wiped her eyes. 'Will you stay here then?'

'Yes, I have a two-day pass.' He rose and patted her shoulder. 'I'll watch over her until you return. Now go home, have something to eat, a bath and sleep. I'll see you tomorrow.'

She nodded, and with a last lingering look at Audrey, she left.

Sighing, Jake sat back on the chair and took Audrey's hand again. 'Can you hear me, Audrey? It's Jake.'

She didn't stir.

'You have to wake up. I've a lot to say to you.' He turned his head as a large nursing sister entered.

'You will have to leave the room, I'm afraid. The doctor is making his rounds now.' She peered at him as though he had two heads or was some criminal from the gutters. 'Are you close family?'

He gave her a penetrating stare. 'I'm Captain Harding, Army doctor, and Miss Pearson's *fiancé*.' He hated lying but needs must. He wasn't having this puffed-up sister dictate to him.

She backed down immediately. 'Ah, well then, that's lovely.' She smiled widely, bustling about the bed, tiding the already tidied sheets. 'Come back in an hour or so, Doctor Harding, and I'll let you sit with her for a while.'

Knowing how regimental hospital rules were, and the grace he'd been given, he reluctantly stood and let go of Audrey's hand. He bent and gently kissed her cheek. 'I love you.'

Outside, he roamed the hospital's limited gardens, which were mainly lawns and the odd tree. For a while he sat on a low stone wall and watched the people coming and going. It was such a busy place, and no one took notice of him as he sat alone with his thoughts.

Audrey had survived a bomb blast and being buried beneath rubble for hours. He'd been so close to losing another good woman who loved him. But this time he'd been given a second chance. Who was he to turn away from her? The bomb had been the wake up call he needed. His old dreams of being a husband and father resurfaced after being buried along with Marianne and their baby. This time things would be different.

He jerked to his feet. Energy sizzled through his veins. He'd take this chance — take it and wring from it every last ounce of happiness he could.

Bounding along the paths back to the entrance, he felt alive again for the first time in years. Alive and impatient to start again, to see Audrey smile at him with love in her eyes. He wanted her in his life. He wanted her love to fill the part of him that had been missing.

Please, God, don't take her from me. I need her more than you.

In the corridor, he halted on seeing the doctor, the sister and a nurse huddled outside of Audrey's room. His heart plummeted to his boots and back up again to lodge in his throat.

No...

As if in a dream, he slowed and focused on the doctor's face, which was frowning.

'I believe you are a doctor in the army?' Audrey's doctor held out his hand and shook Jake's.

'Yes. Jake Harding.' He swallowed the lump in his throat.

'I'm Doctor Burstall.'

'Aud-Audrey is she…is she…'

'You'll be pleased to know your fiancé opened her eyes just a moment ago and spoke.'

The relief mixed with shock buckled his knees. He'd not been ready for that. Awake! Spoken? He rushed into the room.

'Ah, Doctor Harding, she's sleeping now.' Burstall followed him in, trailed by the sister and nurse. 'She was only awake for a moment or two. She asked for water and once Sister wet her lips, she went back to sleep.' He beamed as though he'd performed a miracle. 'I have every confidence she'll be resting naturally now. Of course, we'll monitor her every half hour until she wakes again, and we can access her more thoroughly.'

Jake gazed at her face and noted the subtle change. A little colour had seeped into her skin. 'May I stay with her?' he murmured.

Burstall rocked on his heels. 'Well now—'

'I'm a doctor, I can monitor her better than anyone,' he defended, but catching the eye of the sister, he calmed down. 'If I watch Miss Pearson, it frees up your nursing staff.'

'I can't permit you to be here all night.'

'Of course, you can, if it's your shift.'

Sister cleared her throat and Burstall glanced her way. 'Indeed, it's against all hospital rules…' He twitched his nose and coughed. 'But I don't see the harm in it. Naturally, my nursing staff will still do their duty—'

'Thank you. I appreciate it.' Jake turned his back to them, bringing the subject to a close. He didn't want the doddering old fool to change his mind. No one could look after his Audrey as well as he could.

Throughout the night, he kept his silent vigil, letting her sleep and recover. The nurses kept checking in without disturbing him and the Sister even brought him in a cup of tea.

Just before dawn, Jake put his head on his folded arms that rested on the edge of the bed. His eyes were gritty with tiredness. Sleep had been a rare thing in the last two days. He'd have five minutes rest…

With a jerk he sat up and a pain shot straight down both arms. He blinked and tried to focus on Audrey's face. He'd fallen asleep!

'I bet your neck hurts,' she whispered.

He blinked again. She was awake. 'Aud—' He cleared his throat. 'Audrey.'

Her lips lifted in a slight smile. 'So, it seems.'

Suddenly nervous, Jake took her hand. He studied her, the doctor in him coming to the fore again. 'How do you feel?'

'Fine. The Sister was very pleased with me. My temperature is good, my pulse steady.'

'The Sister? How long have you been awake?'

'Oh, an hour or so.' She frowned. 'Not sure. The sun was up.'

He looked at his watch; ten minutes to eleven. 'I can't believe I slept so long.'

'Nor I in that position.' She grinned. 'The Sister was most concerned about you, as if you were the patient and not I.'

He winked and saw her eyes soften. His heart soared. She still felt something for him.

'How long is your leave?'

'I managed a two-day pass but getting here was a nightmare. I have to return to the hospital this afternoon, as I can't rely on the trains working well enough for me to stay longer.' He took a deep breath and let it out slowly.

'Thank you for coming. I was so surprised to see you beside my bed.'

'Nothing would have stopped me. Don't doubt me.' Gripping her hand tighter, he brought it up to his lips and kissed it. 'I know I've not always given you hope and that doubting me would be easy.'

'Shh, you don't have to say anything.' She yawned and her eyes grew heavy.

'Audrey.'

'Mmm?'

'When you're well again and—' He was interrupted by the arrival of the doctor and a small team of nurses. Under his breath, he swore like a trooper.

Chapter Fourteen

Standing by the window, Audrey watched the busy grounds of the hospital. Behind her on the bed was a small case all packed and ready. Soon Lucy would arrive, and they would travel back home on the train, back to reality and the problems waiting for them.

In the last three days since the bombing, she'd been insulated from the world by this room and the excellent care of the nurses and Doctor Burstall. But with nothing to do except lay in bed, she couldn't help but to think of the future. Her own future was undecided, however, deep in her heat, she knew Jake wouldn't forsake her. Unfortunately, she'd slept most of the time he was by her bed, but the one time they spoke, she'd seen a change in him. Love shone from his eyes, and, for the moment, that was enough for her to hope that one day they'd be together.

It was strange how with her one main worry now reduced, another had come to take its place. In the last two days, Lucy had visited her, yet refused to discuss her 'problem' until Audrey was well again. And so today they would go home, and the life would once again be dealt with. Lucy may have wanted to ignore what lay ahead but she hadn't. Lying in a hospital bed gave you plenty of time to ponder.

Movement to her left made her frown. Was that her father's car? Yes, there was Owen in the front driving the blue and black Daimler into the car park. In amazement, she watched Lucy climb from the back seat and enter the hospital.

Within moments Lucy stood in the doorway, her face overbright, her manner too excited. 'Here we are. Time for you to return to us.'

Audrey remained by the window. 'How did you manage to come by car? I was quite prepared to go home by train.'

'No one would hear of it. Everyone pitched in with their petrol rations so you could come home in comfort.'

'Who is everyone?'

Lucy bounced towards the bed and collected Audrey's bag. 'Friends. Now are you ready? All signed out and what-not?'

Stiff with distrust, Audrey stepped away from the window and followed her eager sister out of the room. 'Are you saying some family friends sent us their petrol rations?'

'Uh-huh.' Lucy nodded, curls waving about her head. 'Come on, Owen is busting his suspenders waiting to see you. Mrs Graham has cooked a feast and Alf—'

'Which particular friends sent the rations?' Audrey peered at Lucy, but her sister wouldn't keep still for a moment and hurried out of the hospital and to the car park. There, Owen sprang from the car, his grin wide and welcoming.

'How wonderful of you to drive all this way, Owen.'

'Nay, Miss.' He stowed her bag in the back and opened the door for her. 'It was a pleasure, Miss. We're all so glad to see you well again.'

She sat in the back. 'Thank you.'

Lucy opened the front passenger door. 'I'll sit in the front with Owen, Audrey. That way you'll have plenty of room.' She climbed in. 'Come along, Owen let us get dear Audrey home to rest.'

All the way home Audrey fidgeted; a sense of unease pounded her head. Lucy's caginess drove her mad. Something was wrong and she couldn't rest until she knew what it was.

By the time Owen pulled the car to a stop, her head throbbed with a spectacular headache. Lucy's prattling set her teeth on edge. After thanking the staff for their warm welcome, she asked Mrs Graham for an Aspirin and headed upstairs.

Her bedroom hadn't changed, but Audrey felt she had. She touched personal items on her dressing table, a bottle of perfume, her jewellery. Unpinning her hat, she turned to her bed and stopped. Poking out from under Lucy's bed was a suitcase handle. Audrey bent and pulled the case out. In two clicks of the locks, she had it open. Lucy's clothes filled it. Blind panic made her heart race. Lucy was leaving. Her headache worsened and she fought the nausea that broke a sweat out onto her body.

When the door opened, Audrey stared up into Lucy's pale face. 'Care to tell me what this is all about?'

'You had no right.' Lucy strode into the room and placed the Aspirin powder and a glass of water on the dressing table.

'I have every right.'

Lucy crossed her arms and raised her chin. 'Yes, I am leaving.'

'Why?'

'I thought that would be obvious.'

'And by leaving what do you hope to achieve?'

'I don't want people around here knowing my business. I'm going away so there will be no gossip.'

Audrey pressed a hand to her stomach. 'I thought we'd discuss all the options together.'

'I've made my decision. It's better this way.'

'For whom?' Audrey snapped. 'For you? For Ralph Dolton?'

Lucy swung away and made for the door. 'I don't want to talk about it.'

'Don't you dare leave this room.' Audrey advanced, ready to pull her back by her hair if need be. 'What happened while I was in the hospital? And he was the one who gave you the petrol rations, wasn't it? The truth now.'

By the door, Lucy faltered. She stared down at her brown shoes, her hands playing with the skirt of her blue dress. 'The truth isn't pretty.'

'It isn't always, but it's better than lies.'

'Ralph Dolton gave me the rations, so what?'

'Why would he do that? Did you tell him about the baby?'

'Yes.'

'And?'

'He doesn't want me…or the child.'

Audrey's stomach twisted in agony for the sadness in her sister's face. 'Oh, dearest.'

'It's what I expected.' Lucy shrugged. 'I'm not good enough for him.'

'Rubbish! You're a damn sight too good for him. The filthy, low life bloody—'

'Don't!' Lucy shouted, her face screwing in anguish. 'Don't say those words about him!'

'How can you defend him after all he's done? Does he think giving you petrol rations to being me home will be enough to ease his conscience? I'd have walked before accepting his help. And here you are defending him again. Lord, Lucy I could slap you silly sometimes.'

'I'm not defending him. I just don't want to hear you call him names.'

'He deserves that and a lot more.'

'I know, but you can't do it.'

'Why, for heaven's sake?'

'Because my baby has him for a father.'

Audrey closed her eyes. Yes, that scoundrel would forever be linked to their family. The realisation of it made the nausea grow. She sat on the bed and held her arms out. 'Come here.'

Lucy ran and threw herself into Audrey's embrace. 'I'm sorry.'

'Shh now.' She placed Lucy beside her and pushed wayward curls out of her eyes. 'Now listen to me. You aren't leaving. I had a lot of time to think while in the hospital.'

'How can I stay?'

'Tell me what you want to do.'

'I don't know…'

'Do you want the baby?'

Lucy shrugged. 'I can't have it on my own. The disgrace…'

'Yes, you will be talked about, and yes we'll lose friends and acquaintances. There will always be gossip.' Lucy groaned but Audrey continued. 'The child will grow up with a stigma and there will be times when it reminds you too much of your mistake, but the alternative is to give it up for adoption and never see it again. Which do you think will be easier to bear?'

'If I give the baby up, it will have a new family without the stigma to worry about.'

'Except the adoption stigma will replace it. The child will always wonder who its parents are.'

'What would you do?'

'I would keep it and deal with any problems as they arise.'

'You make it sound too easy.' Lucy looked away.

'No, it's not.' Audrey took Lucy's chin and made her look at her. 'Whatever decision you choose, it will be the hardest one you'll ever make. But know this. I will always fully support you.'

Lucy bent down and picked up a lacy blouse from the opened suitcase. 'I was going to go to London, find a flat, a job and when the baby came give it away.'

'Do you still want to do that?'

'No. Not now I've spoken to you.' Lucy threw the blouse onto the bed. 'I was leaving tonight. I knew I had to go before I talked to you because you'd change my mind.'

'I'm not changing your mind. You're a woman now and old enough to make your own choices in life. Go if you want. I'll visit you from time to time.'

'Or stay and live with gossip all my life?'

Audrey nodded. 'Yes, but you'll not be alone.'

'I can't think.' Lucy jumped up and paced the floor. 'It's all so hard. I never wanted any of this to happen.'

'I know.'

The shrill of the telephone ringing came from downstairs. Lucy looked at her. 'It'll be Captain Harding for you. He said he would telephone.'

Audrey smiled, love filling her heart. 'I'll call him back later.'

'But—'

'There is no but. This is more important right now.'

Lucy became wistful. 'You love him, don't you? Truly love him.'

'The first time I saw him something in my soul told me that he was the man I could love. Jake knows I love him. He's never been in doubt about that.'

'What makes you so sure he is the one for you?'

'It feels right in here.' Audrey tapped her chest.

'I think he's in love with you too.'

The ringing stopped. 'Hopefully, yes.'

'Will you marry him?'

'When he is ready, I will.'

'How long will that take?'

'Who can tell? He has a past to deal with before he feels safe to give his love to another.'

'What if he's never ready?'

Audrey shivered inwardly at the thought. 'Then we'll have to part ways.'

'He's a good man. Father liked him.'

'Well, we can talk about me and Jake another time. Right now, we need to concentrate on you.'

'I've decided...' Lucy stood still, her shoulders back, head held high. 'I'm keeping my baby.'

'We have another six months or so before you have to make a final decision, dearest.' Audrey rose and rubbed her forehead. The headache was still there, but not as sharp. 'Until then, there'll be no more thoughts of running away, understand?'

'It's not going to be easy.'
'No, it isn't, but we have each other.'

Chapter Fifteen

'I hate Christmas in war time.' On her knees, Lucy swept up the fallen pine needles from the hall floor. Owen and Alf had just brought the Christmas tree in and left a trail of needles all the way into the drawing room.

Audrey wrapped the coloured paper chain around the banister. 'Christmas will be difficult this year. It's just the two of us.'

'No father to hand out presents.'

'Mrs Graham won't be here either. Her nephew has been given leave and she's going to Beverly to spend Christmas with her brother's family.'

Lucy looked up with mischief in her eyes. 'We are left to cook our own food?'

Grimacing, Audrey nodded. 'Yes, sadly. It won't be much of a feast since neither of us can cook very well.'

'Good thing it is only the two of us. Though we could always go to Owen's house. I doubt his Irene would mind, she has Alf for the day, what's two more?'

Audrey laughed. 'I think we can manage.'

Pausing in her sweeping, Lucy tilted her head to one side. 'Actually, it might be nice with just the two of us. We can have a small dinner and listen to the wireless.'

'And play cards or dominoes.'

'Do we have enough food to see us through for a few days? I quite like the idea of us being by ourselves.'

'I'm certain Mrs Graham will have seen that we won't starve.' Audrey winked.

'Are you disappointed that Jake couldn't get leave?'

'Yes, of course, but there's no point getting upset over it. We can't change it. When he telephoned yesterday, I knew he was sorry he couldn't come.'

'And he sends you such lovely letters.'

Thinking of the letters made Audrey glow inside with a warmth she never expected. Jake's letters weren't exactly love letters, but his sentiments and style were such that it left her in no doubt he had feelings for her and that slowly his ghosts were being laid to rest. She would do without him at Christmas if it meant they had the rest of their lives together.

'I'll go and ask Mrs Graham if she needs anything from town before she leaves. I can take the car.' Lucy rose from the floor and her slightly rounded stomach became more prominent despite the loose-fitting woollen dress she wore.

'You want to go to town?'

'I know we decided that I wouldn't go about in public that much now, but I haven't been for weeks and there are a few things I need to do.'

'Ask Owen to drive you. There was ice this morning and the roads will be slippery. It's awfully chilly out there so wear your thick coat and scarf.'

'Will do.' Lucy came up the stairs and kissed Audrey's cheek. 'I'll get some more wool, too, if I can. If nothing else, we can knit.'

'Yes, good idea. Be careful now.' Left alone, Audrey continued twisting the paper chain around the banister. Although they were making the house look festive, in her heart she couldn't find the joy to match it. The baby secret weighed heavily on them both, but they had agreed that for now, it would be best to hide the pregnancy until Lucy was sure in her mind what she wanted to do. She still spoke of keeping the baby, but Audrey believed she was expecting Dolton to arrive with a marriage offer.

At the thought of him, Audrey clenched her teeth. The scoundrel. He'd not been in touch since Lucy told him the news. In fact, Robert had been more of a friend to Lucy than smarmy Dolton. Robert called once a week to have a cup of tea with them and tell them the latest news from Bridlington. They looked forward to his visits. He was the only one to call on them now. So many of their former friends had gone to war and never returned and their parents' friends were of another generation.

With a sigh, she completed the chain twisting. Maybe she and Lucy should go to Owen's house for Christmas Day, anything would be better than moping in the house alone, where their worries could intrude so quickly.

She walked up the last remaining steps, crossed the landing and headed down the end of the hallway. Passing each quiet bedroom, she remembered past Christmas's when there had been such laughter and fun. Now the empty bedrooms reminded her of a time that had ended, of the people missing from her life.

She wiped her eyes of sudden tears. She missed her family and of what had once been such a happy and full home. Why was she so emotional today? She had to snap out of it for Lucy's sake. At the end of the hallway, she climbed the steep narrow stairs leading up to the attics. Opening the door, the smell of staleness hit her, that and the intense cold.

Shivering, she made her way past the cot beds left from when the nurses slept there, and down to the far end where a partition separated the nurses' quarters and the storage area. Amongst the old furniture and boxes were tea chests and crates containing years of family memorabilia. Sorting through them, she found the box of Christmas tree decorations and moving it to one side she uncovered another carton, which held the rolls of film and slides from her father's passion of photography and motion pictures.

It had been years since they had held a slide night. Not since before her mother became ill. She put the carton on top of the other box and searched for the slide projector.

'So, this is where you're hiding?'

Audrey jumped and smothered a scream with her hand. She stared, wide eyed at the one person she didn't expect to see.

Jake stood there and smiled. His manner unsure and slightly vulnerable. 'Surprise.'

The tears that had threatened all day spilled, and she ran into his arms. He hugged her tight and the feel of his embrace, of having his solidness to lean on, outweighed everything in her life at that moment.

He pulled back enough to kiss her hard, a desperate kiss of longing and ownership and she gloried in it, accepting and returning it fully.

When at last they paused for breath, she couldn't help but smile and cry at the same time. 'How did you get leave?'

'Luckily one of the older doctors, Doctor Collins, swapped with me. He has no family and was tired of listening to me whinging about not being here with you.' He winked and kissed her. 'He offered to swap, and I accepted quickly before he could change his mind. Within an hour I was on the train.'

She kissed and held him close. 'My thanks to the good Doctor Collins.'

Looking over her shoulder, he nodded towards the mess surrounding them. 'It took me ten minutes to find you once I'd arrived. What are you doing?'

'I had to find the Christmas decorations, and I also found Father's old slides. I thought Lucy and I could watch them tonight.'

'Is it all right for me to stay too?'

She pushed at his chest playfully. 'What a question. How long is your leave?'

'Four days starting tomorrow, though the fourth day will be travelling back to London.'

'So long!' She did a little jig in his arms. 'How wonderful.'

Jake tightened his hold, and the smile left his face. 'I have three full days to show you how much you mean to me.'

'No doubts?'

He shook his head. 'Not anymore. Spending all these months without you proved to me that the love you offer cannot be ignored. I'm not man enough to

200

walk away from you. I tried to tell you in the hospital, but the time never came for me to do so.'

Audrey cupped his face in her hands and kissed his lips. 'I love you.'

'And I love you.'

'Truly?'

He lightly touched her lips with his fingertip. 'Utterly, absolutely, totally.'

Her whole being melted into a pool of yearning. She couldn't describe her thoughts, which were a jumble of happiness, nor her feelings, which were swooping and whirling with delight that finally the man she loved now loved her in return. 'Oh, Jake.'

'I'm not saying I'll always be perfect, and there will be times when my memories might affect me, but my past won't stop me from loving you or living a complete life.'

She took his cap off and placed it on a box. 'It hasn't been easy for you, I know that.'

'Definitely not easy. There were times I thought I'd go mad.' His gaze became tender and loving. 'But you had managed to hook yourself into my heart and I couldn't rip you out.'

'Do you want to now?' She frowned. 'I don't want you to pretend to save my feelings. Honesty is needed at all times.'

'Never fear, my love,' he kissed her, 'you're mine for ever now whether you like it or not.'

She wound her arms around his neck. 'Oh, I'll like it, that's for certain.'

Jake laughed and hoisted her up. 'Kiss me.'

She lowered her head, chuckling, and kissed him sweetly. 'How was that?'

'Perfect.' He slowly released her back to the floor. 'It's bloody freezing in here. Can we find a fire somewhere?'

'You're too spoilt.' She elbowed him and grinned. 'Help me out with this lot.'

'Already ordering me around.' He stooped and collected the box and carton. 'Is this what my life will be?'

Audrey paused in picking up the projector and stared at him. 'We're going to be together long term?'

His eyes widened. 'Of course! What did you think I meant?'

'I wasn't sure. I didn't want to think so far ahead.'

Over the boxes and equipment, he kissed her check, her neck and lastly the tip of her nose. 'You wanted me, my love, now you have me. Forever. As I love and want you.'

She sighed in complete happiness. Never had she thought she'd really get all that she wanted. 'Then after the war…'

'After the war, we'll spend the rest of our lives together either here at Twelve Pines or wherever you wish.'

'Thank you.'

'No, thank you for allowing me to live again.' He winked again to lighten the seriousness and then shivered. 'Christ, it's cold in here.'

~ ~ ~

'It's going to be an excellent Christmas. I just know it.' Lucy clapped as Audrey opened the decorations box and handed her a paper angel to put on the tree.

'You don't mind that Jake is here? I know you wanted it to be just the two of us.'

Lucy reached up and attached the angel. 'Yes, well, we had no choice, did we? It was going to be us whether we wanted it or not, and so I thought to make the best of it.'

'He means so much to me, Lucy.'

'I can see that, silly.' Lucy giggled and reached for another decoration. 'I'm so happy that you're so happy.' She fingered the painted pinecone. 'We've not had anything to celebrate in such a long time. I think we deserve it, don't you?'

'We do indeed.'

'There will be no happy ending for me with Dolton.'

'That is definite?'

'Yes. I heard this morning in town that Dolton's gone to America with his new fiancée.'

'Fiancée?' Audrey gasped. Even though she hated the man she always hoped he'd arrive, beg forgiveness and do the right thing by Lucy.

Lucy let out a long breath. 'Good riddance to bad rubbish, I say.'

'Oh Luce.'

'I don't mind all that much, not as much as I thought I would.'

'Who told you?'

'Nancy Phillips. Apparently, his fiancée is also expecting, but he picked her because she has wealthy family connections in New York, and I know Ralph always wanted to be an important man in New York. Here's his chance.'

'Dearest…'

'No, it's no bother. I'll survive. I really haven't missed him, would you believe? I imagine I didn't like him as much as I thought I did.'

'You don't need him. You have me, and now you have Jake too.'

'Yes, and it's more than enough. I'm very lucky. Some families throw their daughters out of the house in such circumstances. Would Father have done that to me?'

'No, father adored you too much and he was far more broad-minded than others of his generation.' Audrey passed another painted pinecone. 'Did Nancy suspect about you?'

'No. Not at all. I didn't talk to her long, as Robert saw me across the street and came over. We went for a cup of tea.'

'Lord!' Audrey smacked her forehead. 'We should have invited Robert for Christmas. What were we thinking of?'

Lucy laughed. 'I know. I realised that this morning. So, I invited him.' She blushed. 'I hope you don't mind.'

Relieved, Audrey knelt back on her heels. 'Oh good. Yes, that is perfect really. Evens the numbers out and he is so jolly, always smiling.'

'And he's by himself. We couldn't let him spend Christmas alone.'

Audrey rose and dusted down her brown skirt. 'I'll check on Jake, poor man. We shouldn't have left him in the kitchen to do all the work.'

'He offered to wash up.'

'Yes, and we also helped to eat the lunch Mrs Graham left us.'

'Is Jake really going to cook our dinner tomorrow?'

Grinning, Audrey paused by the door. 'Yes, and he said he can even make custard to go with that apple pie Mrs Graham made.'

'Oh, a man that can cook. You have to marry him, Aud.'

'Yes, there are some good things about the army.' Laughing, Audrey left the drawing room, which had been restored to its former comfort, and headed for the kitchen. There, she found Jake putting away plates. 'I've come to help.'

'Huh, a little late, sweetheart.' He kissed her as she passed. 'All the hard work has been done.'

'My timing is perfect then.' She smiled up at him and sat at the table. 'Now, are you positive you can handle dinner tomorrow?'

He raised an eyebrow. 'You don't have much confidence in me, do you?'

'Well, Lucy and I can't cook, or at least not very well, so we will be depending on your talents to feed us.'

'And here was I, hoping for a rest over Christmas.'

She stood and wrapped her arms around his waist. 'I promise that aside from cooking, you'll not have to do another thing but kiss me.'

He looked thoughtful. 'I think I can manage that request.'

'Show me, my good man.' She wiggled in his arms and laughed as he savaged her neck like a madman.

Much later, after playing about, kissing, chatting and holding each other, Jake returned to his kitchen duties and Audrey acted as his assistant. A comfortable silence descended while Jake cut slices of bread for their supper and she made a fresh pot of tea.

'Audrey?'

'Hmm?' She glanced up from measuring out the tea leaves.

'We'll always be honest with each other, won't we?'

Lowering the spoon, she turned to see him fully. 'Of course.'

Jake gaze remained steady. 'Then why haven't you told me about Lucy expecting a baby?'

'How did you know?'

'It might have something to do with me being a doctor, or the fact her stomach is quite rounded, and I heard her bringing up her breakfast the other morning.'

Audrey sagged against the bench. 'I…Please don't think I was deceiving you intentionally. I mean, I wanted to tell you, but I had to ask Lucy first. Your arrival was so unexpected. We haven't told anybody.'

He crossed the floor to take her hands. 'I'm not accusing you of keeping secrets.' His blue eyes softened. 'Do you feel you can tell me anything?'

'Yes, absolutely.'

'Good.'

'Do you?'

'Oh, yes. I've already told you things no one else knows.' He kissed her hands. 'So, Lucy is having a child.'

'I still can't really believe it. I was so shocked, Jake. I didn't know what to think or do.'

'Why didn't you confide in me?'

She sighed and rubbed her eyes. 'To be honest, it took so long for us to come to terms with the news, that I presumed we tried to believe it would all go away, but that, of course, is silly.'

'Is Lucy giving it up for adoption?'

'No…'

'Then the father will marry her?'

Shaking her head, she turned back to the teapot. 'She wants to keep it, and I said I'd help her.'

'Keep it?' He came to stand beside her at the sink. 'Have you thought this through and what it'll mean?'

'Naturally. We've done nothing else but think about it. The last few months have been such a torment.'

Jake rested his back on the bench next to the sink. 'It will be extremely tough, Audrey. There'll be gossip and name calling, being shunned—'

'We know all that.' She scooped more tea leaves into the pot and then poured in the boiling water. 'The alternative is to give the child away and forever wonder about it. Would that be easier? I think not.'

'It will be on the child.'

She set out the tray with cups and saucers, sugar bowl and spoons. Next, she poured milk into the small jug and set that onto the tray too.

Jake straightened and faced her. 'Once we are married, would you like us to adopt the baby?'

She spun so fast she knocked over the milk jug, sending milk flowing across the table. 'Marriage.'

'You don't want marriage?' He frowned. 'I'm all for you being independent, but I had thought one day you'd want to marry me, warts and all.'

She flung herself into his arms and hugged him tightly. 'Of course, I want to marry you, I love you!'

With a huge sigh, he grinned. 'That's a relief, I thought you were going to turn me down.'

'Why would I do that?' She kissed him hard and quick. 'Haven't I given you enough proof that I want to spend the rest of my life with you?'

Jake rested his forehead against hers. 'We'll be all right, the two of us.'

'I know.'

'But there is one thing that concerns me.'

'Oh?'

'I'm frightened of you being pregnant. After Marianne, the notion of it happening to you scares me witless. Even seeing Lucy with child makes me wince, and I hope it all goes well for her, I truly do, but it just brings back such painful memories. If it were to happen to you...'

She cupped her hands on either side of his face. 'Darling, I'm not Marianne. We are two different people, with different bodies. Look how healthy I am. And my hips...' she did a wiggle in his arms. 'Wide enough for a hundred babies.'

Grinning, he pulled her closer. 'I know not every woman dies in childbirth, but I can't help being worried.'

'I understand, darling, I do, but it won't happen to me, I won't let it.'

'It's out of your hands, even doctors—'

'Shh...' She silenced him with a kiss. 'Our life together will be just fine. I know it in my heart.'

'I meant what I said about Lucy's baby.'

Blinking in surprise, Audrey stepped back. 'You really mean it? What you're asking is not something we can agree to lightly.'

'True, but it might be the answer for both Lucy and the child. Think it over anyway and talk to Lucy.'

'I can't believe you would offer to do such a thing.'

'Why?'

'To adopt another man's child...' She stared at him, loving him completely.

'Sweetheart, it's not the child's fault. In my line of work, I've seen so many unhappy children, it breaks my heart that I can't help them all. This child can have a mother and father that are directly related to him or her.'

'I would hate to see the baby given away and never knowing about it again.'

'Who is the father?'

'Ralph Dolton. He used Lucy terribly and she was too immature and infatuated to see it.'

'It happens regularly. She has no contact with him?'

'No.' For a moment Audrey remembered another time she and Jake had discussed another young woman alone and pregnant, Nurse Peters. She also remembered the argument she had with Jake over it. 'Do you think badly of Lucy now?'

'No, Dolton was older. He should have been a gentleman, but it's not in that man's character.'

She nodded and nibbled her fingernail. 'I'll discuss it with Lucy. It is her decision.'

'Well, while she's thinking it over, we can arrange our wedding. Yes?'

'Yes.' She grinned and took his hand. 'What about your mother? I'll have to meet her. Will she like me?'

For a moment he studied the soft skin of her wrist. 'I spoke to Mother when I saw her last. She knows about you and insisted on meeting you. She's getting old, Audrey, and wants her family around her.'

'I want to meet her. Invite her here, Jake. She can spend a week here getting to know me.'

'Really?' A light flared in his eyes. 'You'd do that?'

'Why wouldn't I want to know my mother-in-law?'

'Marianne didn't.' He lifted one shoulder in a small shrug. 'I'm sorry. The past is past.'

'Yes, it is. Don't think of me as another Marianne, I beg you. I'm Audrey Pearson, and I want to get to know your mother.'

'I'll promise to try to not compare you, and I haven't been, really. It's just sometimes the past can ride my shoulder a bit.'

'I know, my love, but we'll meet any challenges together.'

'Thank you, it means a lot to me.'

Kissing her, holding her close, he made her feel special, worthy and terribly loved. 'Did I tell you I love you?' she whispered.

'Did I tell you I haven't bought you a ring yet?' He grinned and ducked when she hit him on the shoulder.

'Why you!'

Laughing, Jake wrapped his arms around her waist and lifted her off the floor. 'After Christmas and before I return to London, we'll go into Bridlington and I'll buy you a ring.'

She sighed happily and leaned against his shoulder. This was a man worth loving.

~ ~ ~

In the flickering candlelight, Audrey sat back and breathed in deeply. She'd eaten too much Christmas dinner. Jake had cooked a superb roast chicken with the last of the garden vegetables. Outside, the cold weather had kept them indoors all day, but they didn't mind. After Robert arrived this morning, the four of them opened presents. With the wireless on in the background they'd played cards and dominoes, eaten cakes, drank tea. The telephone rang a few times with family friends sending their greetings, but other than that, they'd been left alone to enjoy a quiet but contented Christmas day.

She fingered the sapphire and diamond pendant hanging on a gold chain around her neck. Jake's present had brought tears to her eyes when she opened it. She reached for her wine and sipping it, she gazed at the three people sitting at the table. Because of the cold, they decided to eat in the kitchen where it was warm.

Jake cleared his throat. 'I have an announcement.'

Audrey looked at him and he winked.

Robert and Lucy stopped talking and turned their attention to him, Lucy wore a confused expression.

'Lucy, Robert, yesterday I asked Audrey to marry me and she accepted.'

Lucy squealed, jumped and hugged Audrey, crying happy tears while Robert nearly shook Jake's hand off.

'I'm so pleased for you both.' Lucy wiped her eyes. 'Audrey has been in love with you since you arrived here back in March.'

'Lucy!' Audrey blushed. 'Hush your tongue. Will you ever change?'

Robert held up his glass. 'To the happy couple.'

They all rose and clinked glasses. Audrey's heart swelled with emotion. She didn't have her parents or brother to share the moment, but she had Lucy and now Jake. Life went on and she'd live it to the best of her ability.

'There's apple pie and custard.' Jake picked up her plate.

She took Lucy and Robert's plates. 'Sit down, Jake. I'll wash up and Lucy can help. She's done nothing all day but eat.' Audrey grinned.

Lucy, talking to Robert, stopped mid-sentence. 'Let us have dessert in the drawing room in front of the fire for once.'

'I'll help tidy away.' Robert began clearing the table.

'No, Robert,' Jake stalled him. 'Audrey and I can clear away. You take Lucy into the drawing room and stir the fire up. We'll spend the night in there.'

Lucy stepped to Jake and kissed him. 'You are going to make a very good brother!' Chuckling and blowing a kiss to Audrey she left the room with Robert.

'Don't you start spoiling her.' Audrey gave Jake stern look. 'She's been spoilt all her life.'

He placed the plates on the bench. 'I always wanted a little sister.'

She threw a napkin at him and for the next half hour they spent more time being silly than cleaning but neither of them cared a whit.

Later, sitting curled up on the sofa in Jake's arms, Audrey wondered if she could be any more blissful than at that moment. They spent the evening dancing to music on Lucy's gramophone until Lucy was exhausted. Audrey had invited Robert to stay the night and he'd gone upstairs to bed the same time Lucy did, obviously to give her and Jake time alone.

The only sound was the crackle of the logs on the fire and its golden glow provided the only light. Audrey's eyes grew heavy as good food and dancing took its toll on her.

'You're not falling asleep or you?' Jake whispered down at her, where she lay beside him.

'No...' She yawned behind her hand and grinned.

He kissed the top of her head. 'I don't want today to end.'

'A beautiful day.'

'The best.'

'I never thought it would be, not a few months ago. What with Lucy's predicament, and then our first Christmas without any family with us. I was dreading it.'

'Come here.' Jake gathered her up onto his lap and she snuggled against his chest. 'You know, I think Lucy and Robert have hit it off. Robert never takes his eyes of Lucy.'

'Yes, I know.' She fidgeted with the buttons of his army shirt. 'But he doesn't know about the baby. That will change things.'

'Maybe not.' Running his fingers through her curls, Jake stared at the flames. 'Not every man runs away from responsibility.'

'Mmm, I guess so.' She popped one of his buttons and slipped her fingers inside his shirt. 'We'll have to see what comes of it.'

'Yes…' Jake lowered his head to capture her mouth. His free hand ran down her leg sending shivers through her. She worked on the other buttons and freed his shirt from his trousers.

'Audrey…' Jake voice deepened; his movements more hurried.

She kissed his chest, her tongue circling one nipple and he tensed a moment, then slowly undid the buttons on her blouse and eased it open to stroke her breast beneath her lacy white bra. His magnificent blue eyes spoke a language of their own and she arched into his touch.

'Love me properly, Jake. I can't wait any longer.'

Groaning, he buried his face in her neck, his hands creating magic with his caresses. 'I don't think I can say no, sweetheart.'

She smiled and ran her fingers through his hair. 'I never want to hear you say no again.'

Epilogue

May 1946

Audrey raised her head from gazing at the baby in her arms to the sunshine. She closed her eyes and wondered if she was dreaming. Was it possible to be this happy? Her life was everything she hoped it would be. She had married Jake in March last year, and when the war finished, he opened a doctor's practice in Bridlington. He'd also gone into partnership with Robert, who opened a mechanics garage to fix motorcars.

Throughout her pregnancy, Jake had pretended he wasn't overly concerned for her safety, but she'd known by the nightmares that disturbed his sleep how badly he suffered. However, the end result had been worth it. Oliver's birth lasted ten hours and without complication. Indeed, only an hour after his birth, she was begging for a cup of tea and a bowl of Mrs Graham's beef broth. When Jake realised she was out of danger, the stress left him and together they enjoyed their precious son's arrival.

A bee buzzed near her feet and she watched it for a moment in case it came too close. Her mother's roses bloomed beautifully in the early warmth of May. Although the war had finished a year ago, they still had more vegetables than flowers in the gardens, as rations were to be continued until the country recovered from the effects of five years of upheaval.

Her son gurgled sleepily, and she smiled down at him. 'They'll be home soon, little one.' Gently, she stroked his soft downy head. He possessed his father's features, but his hair was black like hers.

Reaching into her pocket, she pulled out the latest letter from Valerie, who still lived in France, serving at a hospital in Paris. The war-torn capital needed all the aid it could to rebuild and cater for its servicemen and citizens. Valerie wrote at least once a fortnight, filling pages with her neat handwriting and giving Audrey an image of what her world was like now. Only, Audrey missed her, and wanted her home again. Often, she had replied to the letters with one burning question of her own, when was she coming back to England?

Over the sound of the birds singing in the trees and the fountain bubbling in the carp pond, she heard the distant rumble of engines. Her family were returning from Bridlington, where they'd gone to celebrate the first anniversary of the war ending.

Soon the noise of talking and laughter drifted across the gardens, as everyone climbed out of cars and made their way to the picnic area. Her peace was shattered, but she didn't mind. Once, she had worried she'd be left alone at Twelve Pines. Instead, she had gained a whole new family.

Smiling, she watched her mother-in-law, Iris, stroll across the lawns, chatting away to Alf, Owen and his wife. Iris had come to live at Twelve Pines last March when her son had got married. Iris Harding was a formidable woman on the outside, but soft as butter on the inside where it counted, and Audrey had loved her at once. She found it odd that she'd never had a problem living with her mother-in-law, as most people claimed to do. Between them, they lived in harmony. It helped that they had their own interests, but always at night, after dinner, they would retire to the drawing room and talk for hours. Iris had filled the hole in Audrey left by her mother's early departure, and she was grateful for it.

'There you are, my dears,' Iris declared, bending over to kiss Audrey's cheek before doing the same to her grandson's head. 'Everything well?'

'It will be if you take him for a moment.' Audrey chuckled, passing Oliver over. 'He fair weighs a bit when you've been holding him a while.'

'Aye, he's feeding like a little warrior, so he is.' Iris settled into a garden chair and nestled the baby in her arms with a contented sigh. 'Now then, my little chap. You been a good boy for your mother?'

Alf and Owen, with the help of Irene, set out more chairs and Audrey spotted Mrs Graham bearing down on them carrying a loaded tea tray. Behind her, came Lucy carrying another tray of sandwiches. Robert pushed the pram that held baby Tiffany, who at fifteen months old was everyone's darling girl.

'We're home.' Lucy grinned. 'Did you miss us?' She kissed Audrey's cheek. 'How is my delightful nephew?'

'He's fine.' Audrey received Robert's kiss and then tickled Tiffany under the chin. 'Did you all have a good time?'

'Yes, though there were so many people.' Lucy glanced at Robert for confirmation. 'Such crowds weren't they, Robert?'

'It was a good turnout.' Robert, as always gazed adoringly at his wife. They'd married three weeks after that special Christmas Day. On Boxing Day, Lucy had told Robert about her pregnancy and he instantly offered to marry her and claim the child as his. At first, Audrey worried that Lucy rushed into it, but Lucy had assured her that Robert meant something to her, and time had proven that to be true. They made a good couple and just this morning Lucy confided to her that she was expecting again.

Audrey looked beyond them for Jake. 'Where's my husband then? I hope you didn't leave him behind.'

'He's coming. He has a surprise for you.' Lucy didn't appear impressed. 'He's as daft as a brush, and I told him so. I tried talking him out of it, but he wouldn't have it.'

Curious, Audrey rose from her chair. 'I'll go find him and see what he's up to.'

Robert stepped forward and from the basket under the pram brought out his camera equipment. 'There's actually two surprises for you, but I'm sworn to secrecy.'

'Two surprises?' Lucy stared at him. 'What is the other one? How could you not tell me?'

Robert famous grin appeared, and he kissed his wife to silence her.

Audrey shook her head with amusement and walked back to the house. At the doorway to the cloakroom, she stopped and stared at Jake squatting down beside Max's old bed. 'What are you doing?'

He glanced up and grinned, then moved back to show off his treasure. Squirming in the dog basket were two black Labrador puppies. 'I got them for you.'

She blinked. Puppies? She'd just had a baby! 'Jake, I—'

'Now don't worry, I'll train them, so you won't have that bother. Alf and Owen will help. The place needs dogs, they both said so.'

'Those two will tell you anything.' She stepped towards them, smiling as they chewed the basket and each other. 'Where did you get them?'

'From a patient.' He rose and cuddled her to his side. 'Do you like them?'

'Well, yes, but—'

'What shall we call them?'

'I've no idea.'

'They'll be good pets for Oliver.'

She laughed. 'Our son is four weeks old.'

'They'll grow up together.' Jake shrugged.

'You're completely mad.'

He kissed her soundly. 'That is why you love me.'

'Indeed, I do.'

His hands slipped down to cup her bottom. 'I have another surprise.'

She gave him a saucy look. 'Have you now? I was warned about men like you Doctor Harding.'

'Now what are you thinking of Mrs Harding?' he whispered in her ear.

She slapped his shoulder playfully. 'What is this other surprise?'

'Wait here and close your eyes.' Jake left her and she heard him go into the corridor and then walk back. 'Right, you can look now.'

Audrey opened her eyes and looked straight at Valerie. It took a moment for her to register was she saw. 'Val?'

'The one and only.' Val spread her arms wide and Audrey rushed into them, squealing.

For several moments they talked, cried and laughed together, reaffirming their friendship and bond.

'So, I thought I'd better come see my Godson.' Valerie grinned, linking her arm through Audrey's.

'He's so beautiful, Val. I adore him.'

Jake cleared his throat. 'He takes after his father, that's why.'

Audrey reached over and kissed him. 'I'll agree to that. Thank you for my surprises.'

He kissed her softly. 'For you, anything.'

'Shall I go join the others?' Val sniffed in mock disapproval.

Audrey hugged. 'We'll all go and have a wonderful day together. I'm so happy I could burst.'

'No, you were like that carrying Oliver.' Jake joked.

'Oh you!' Audrey stuck out her tongue and linked both her arms through Val and Jake's.

At the door, Jake clicked his fingers. 'Come on you two.' The puppies tumbled out of the basket. 'Come and meet the family.'

When Lucy saw Val, she screamed, and Val ran ahead to embrace her.

Arm in arm, Audrey and Jake ambled back to the group with the puppies bouncing along behind.

Audrey knew the day she met Captain Jake Harding that he was the one for her. Sure, her belief had been shaken, and there were times when the past might have won, but she fought for what she wanted and needed. Jake, once a broken man, was healing and learning it was safe to love again.

He gazed down at her, his blue eyes she adored full of love. 'Are you happy, Mrs Harding?'

'Supremely.' She grinned.

He took her hand and kissed it. 'No regrets?'

'None whatsoever, my love.'

AnneMarie Brear

Australian born, AnneMarie Brear's ancestry is true Yorkshire going back centuries.

Her love of reading fiction started at an early age with Enid Blyton's novels, before moving on into more adult stories such as Catherine Cookson's novels as a teenager.

Her books are available in ebook and paperback from bookstores, especially online bookstores. Please feel free to leave a review online if you enjoyed Broken Hero.

Ms Brear has done it again. She quickly became one on my 'must read' list.
–The Romance Studio

http://www.annemariebrear.com
https://www.facebook.com/annemariebrearauthor
https://twitter.com/annemariebrear

Printed in Great Britain
by Amazon